# PRINCE
# CHARLIE'S
# YEAR

# PRINCE CHARLIE'S YEAR

## JAMES D. FORMAN

CHARLES SCRIBNER'S SONS • NEW YORK

Maxwell Macmillan Canada   Toronto

Maxwell Macmillan International

New York   Oxford   Singapore   Sydney

I can in no way deny a susceptibility to the Jacobite mythology and on this account am more than grateful to the Keeper of the United Services Museum in Edinburgh, Scotland, Stephen Wood, author on his own account of such scholarly works as *The Scottish Soldier* and *The Auld Alliance, Scotland and France: The Military Connection*, for having fulfilled his promise to "savage with unrestrained glee" the overly romantic manuscript. The result, tempered in such fire, is undoubtedly a far more accurate and balanced book.

J.D.F.

Charles Scribner's Sons Books for Young Readers
Macmillan Publishing Company
866 Third Avenue, New York, NY 10022

Maxwell Macmillan Canada, Inc.
1200 Eglinton Avenue East, Suite 200
Don Mills, Ontario M3C 3N1

Macmillan Publishing Company is part of
the Maxwell Communication Group of Companies.

First edition    10  9  8  7  6  5  4  3  2  1
Printed in the United States of America

Library of Congress Cataloging-in-Publication Data
Forman, James D.
Prince Charlie's year / James D. Forman.    p.    cm.
Summary: In 1745 fourteen-year-old Colin joins his father to
fight with Bonnie Prince Charlie in his attempt at the throne.
ISBN 0-684-19242-X
1. Jacobite Rebellion, 1745–1746—Juvenile fiction.
[1. Jacobite Rebellion, 1745–1746—Fiction.
2. Scotland—History—18th century—Fiction.]    I. Title.
PZ7.F76Pr  1991    [Fic]—dc20    90-26898

For two favorite couples just this year married:

Tony and Rachel,
who have much of Charles Edward
and Flora McDonald about them,

and

Sheena and Stephen,
English in origin and hence skeptical,
yet wed in as romantically Scottish a setting
as that Celtic land has to offer.

May these four live happily ever after.

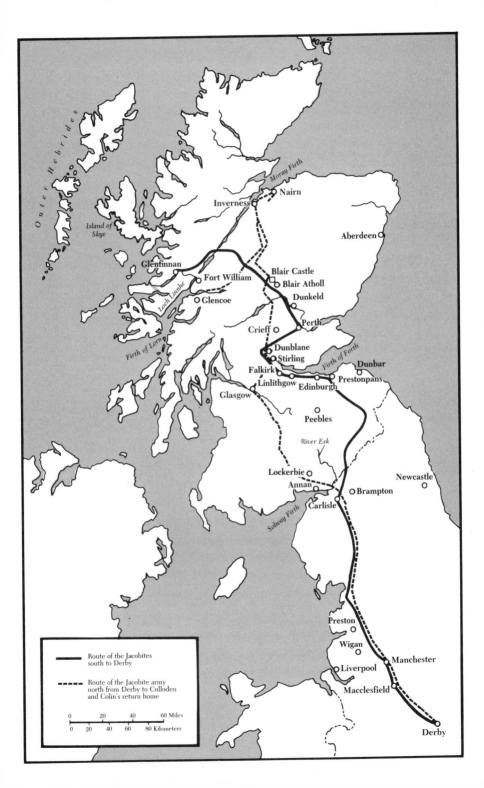

Outer Hebrides

Moray Firth

Nairn

Inverness

Island of Skye

Aberdeen

Glenfinnan

Blair Castle

Fort William

Blair Atholl

Loch Linnhe

Glencoe

Dunkeld

Perth

Crieff

Dunblane

Stirling

Firth of Forth

Dunbar

Falkirk

Linlithgow

Prestonpans

Firth of Lorn

Edinburgh

Glasgow

Peebles

River Esk

Lockerbie

Newcastle

Annan

Brampton

Carlisle

Solway Firth

Preston

Wigan

Manchester

Liverpool

Macclesfield

Route of the Jacobites
south to Derby

Route of the Jacobite army
north from Derby to Culloden
and Colin's return home

0        20        40        60 Miles

0     20    40    60    80 Kilometers

Derby

# 1

On this first day of September in the year of Our Lord 1780, I take pen in hand to confess that I am here in violation of a solemn oath made over thirty years ago never again to take up arms against the king of England. Is there honor and good sense in what I do now? Such is my conviction. Were such qualities part of what I did as a boy? I no longer know and must leave it to whomsoever reads these words to decide for themselves.

The fact remains that for the second time in my life I have left home and loved ones to stand against the redcoats, many of them Scots like myself, and this time they are led by a Scot, a good man for all that I am told, though threatening this land with fire and sword.

Let it be on record that my full name is Colin Randall MacDonald, though I have not used my proper surname since being transported against my will across the ocean. I am now in my forty-ninth year, old as soldiers go, but hardened by the world and all it has done to me, so I am

1

not daunted by a long march or living off the land, nor am I fearful of the battle that awaits I know not where. If you would know me on sight, imagine a lean man of average height, five and a half feet—which is tall for a Scot—long face darkened by so many seasons of farming and hunting under the American sun, and stubbled now since few of us have shaved since leaving home. This beard, I suspect, has obscured my most identifying feature, a long pale scar upon my right cheek, which I have worn with pride since the age of fourteen as a memento of Culloden Moor. You see, I was born in Scotland, at a place known to few. Glencoe is how it is named on some of the larger maps, yet it has darker names: the Valley of the Dogs, for one, or that which it has so well earned in recent years, the Glen of Weeping.

My Peggy says I should forget all that, but forgetting is not something you do, it is something that happens, and it never happened to me. If I close my eyes the beauty returns unbidden: all those tiny streams in spring playing over brightly polished stones to flow into the River Coe, winding down the glen. Then Aonach Eadach rises up from the purple shadows. 'Twas a poor land even then, but lovely beyond words. In stormy weather it could be a fearful place. Once giants lived in the mountains round about, and there are ghosts there still. You may laugh, but I have known them, and they would surely be laughing now could they see me with my rifle marching against King George as I marched against his grandfather long ago.

When I hear that hollow laughter inside me I wonder why I bring up these old stories again. Let the dead rest in peace; yet if I let them rest, they will be as toys played with by children, to be broken and lost, and it is hard to think of one's life—all those lives—carelessly cast away. I may make little sense of my life in this telling. That I will leave to others—my grandchildren, perhaps, when they are old enough, and their children's children. An old rebel's vanity? Perhaps, but if not now, I may not live to tell this story. It seems unwise for a soldier to plan beyond a battle, and I feel still favored by fortune to have survived my fourteenth year. That was "Prince Charlie's Year," and even today I need only lift my eyes toward the sun to see the glimmer of bayonets and muskets raised against me.

It is hardest to recall the years before Charlie came. One year seems so like another, driving the sad-eyed, shaggy black cattle in keeping with the changing seasons. In spring we took them up to the high meadows, which were all ablaze with primroses and hyacinth. With high summer we moved them north onto saw-toothed Aonach Eadach, where the path grew so narrow it was called the Devil's Staircase. By the time I was a boy the wild boar and the wolves had vanished, but wildcats and badgers still roamed. Eagles and kites, linnets and blackbirds swam on the wind, and when autumn came we hunted the red deer for their meat and hides. The west wind brought swans from the Outer Isles, and it was grand for boys until winter came, when it was time to drive the herd down to Loch Achtriachtan or Levenside. Of course the black cattle are gone now, and most of my family, the MacDonalds, as well. My mother, if she lives, may still be there, and my sister, Mary. I sometimes think poor Mary will never die and that, like the lonely ghosts, she is doomed to haunt those hills forever, driving the black cattle before her.

My father was Cluny MacDonald. He is dead these many years, but in those days he was the *Ceann-cinnidh*, the head of our family and a man of some consequence in the clan. He had been to King's College in the city of Aberdeen and was acknowledged to be both bard and piper among the MacDonalds of Glencoe. We were not a great clan in numbers, but our name, it was said, was another word for

3

"proud." As bard, my father wore tartan trews, which were long hose, and buckled shoes like the highborn, not the kilted plaid and deerhide brogues of the common folk. Besides playing the pipes at grand affairs, he had the task as bard to praise the chief and his ancestors, and to keep the records of the clan's deeds down the years from Conn of One Hundred Battles to the Lord of the Isles and the days of his own glory, when he cut down more than one foeman at Sheriffmuir. This last was a tale my father left for others to tell, though he never did deny it.

I can still hear him say, "Laddie, I am not a loving man, but these mountains, this valley . . ." I believe he cared no less for his family and the clan, and he worshiped the Stuart kings with a dangerous passion, likening himself to Rob Gib, the court jester who insisted he alone of all the courtiers loved his monarch selflessly.

My mother, Elspeth, when I knew her, was a lady of stout heart and strong arm. She was born a MacGregor—"children of the mist" as they called themselves after their name was stricken for raiding Campbell cattle and the like. I believe she, too, had the makings of a bard. Many of the songs my father sang were hers, but whereas he saw the glories of the past, she had a gift for seeing through earth and space and telling what would be true in days to come. We Highlanders have a strong belief in second sight, but perhaps being a MacGregor turned my mother's vision to the dark side. She called our Highlands "this black land," with no future for the clans. She was more right than anyone could foretell, although it is strange that, with so many of us flung to the corners of the world, my mother is one of the few abiding there yet.

Unlike the rest of us, my sister Mary was small and her hair was fair. She was frail at first glance but in truth was as tough as the heather and as fleet of foot as a cloud's shadow. I feel sure she dwells in Glencoe yet, and if any of the black cattle have returned, I know she keeps them faithfully through the hard seasons. My sister may not have been beautiful, but she was lovely with her skin as fair as an apple blossom. I think of her as a squirrel nesting in the pine tops. Remembering her laughter still breaks my heart, for it was I who took home the black news of Angus Og Sinclair, the only man in her life.

A word or two more of Angus Og, for he was a friend to my father and a fellow piper, who saw me safely through my dangerous fourteenth year. I will not forget his warm handshake and steady good nature through thick and thin, or even the way he moved like a great cat, every motion with the smooth agility and strength of a body kept fit by constant physical work. When the call came from Charlie, Angus Og should have marched with the mixed clans, for there were not enough Sinclairs to form their own company, but he went with the MacDonalds out of love and because he shared our grievance against the Campbells.

Like his father before him, Angus Og was a fisherman, and in sailing southward to the Firth of Lorn he often encountered Campbell boats. Now, the Campbells are Lowlanders, in their hearts English, not Scots. The Campbells were charged by the English long ago with keeping the peace, and they have done so bloodily and at our expense. Now some would say their reputation is darker than their due, but there were Campbells among those soldiers quartered upon my people during the hard winter of 1692. Yet, under this trust, they rose by night and slaughtered Red Alasdair, the chief, and many of his clan children, driving others forth into a blizzard so no count was ever surely made of those who died. Ever after our home has been called the Glen of Weeping, and in the western Highlands Campbells remain the great foe. Many were the Sinclair and MacDonald lands that have been given over, through the years, to the Campbells, and many a Sinclair and MacDonald neck has been stretched on Inverary's Gallows Hill because of the Campbells. It was for this, and not for love of Charlie, that Angus Og Sinclair heeded the fiery cross when it was borne through the glens.

Finally, and most important to me, there is Angus Og's youngest sister, Peggy, to whom I owe all the happiness I have found in this world. In those days she had the same proud lean look as her brother, the same high-bridged nose and long limbs. She has changed little over the years. I see the same slightly skeptical gray eyes, a skin like pure honey, and the full Sinclair mouth with the upper lip lifted as though in surprise. Her curly hair still hangs down like clusters of grapes.

We were twelve when we first met. Peggy was standing on her father's boat, her legs firmly planted on the planking, looking so much older and so in command of things I scarcely dared speak to her at all. Then came that wide, boyish, honest grin of hers, and we were friends. I think there must have been saltwater in her blood, for she always fancied adventure and far horizons, and though she had no gift of second sight, my Peggy always insisted the Highlands were too cold and the summers of home too short.

It might not have been love at first sight between us, but it was close to that, and I never complained about a market trip to Fort William, since that was where the Sinclairs moored their boat until the prince came home. I learned to like eating fish. I like it still.

Apart from those trips to the loch, which was not far, I seldom left the glen as a boy. Why go elsewhere? I loved my home and thought I knew the future. In time I, too, would master the pipes, perhaps with a summer on the Isle of Skye learning from the master MacCrimmon pipers.

Meanwhile, with my father's help I practiced, and I learned the tales of MacDonald glory, which had been passed down by my grandfather. I remember little of my father's father, save a roaring voice and a rough affection. As a young man he had gone out with MacIain in the '89 rising. Now in his age he described that long-ago chief as a peacock's tail in his splendor. A bard or piper worth his salt—and I include my father and grandfather in this—sings of clan glory and adds to it.

With such ancestors it was easy for a boy to fill up with dreams of daring, banners on the wind and the fierce clang of claymores, a way of life that stretched back endlessly until myth and legend flowed together. It would be my task and pride to pass these tales along. Even my mother dared not guess otherwise, or if she did, she held her tongue.

How can I believe all that is past, cut off from me as finally as the legendary days of the Vikings? There is no going home. The MacDonalds are gone from Glencoe, along with their black cattle. The glen has been left to the sheep. Today I picture Glencoe lit by lightning, never sunshine. Peggy and I were lucky to get away, for the others did not. Their land is dying. This one, if please God we win this last battle, is not. My journal, as the not-quite-last bard of the MacDonalds of Glencoe, is a debt I owe to my family and my clan.

# 2

*Watango River*

SEPTEMBER 22, 1780

One thousand or more "Over Mountain Men" have joined us here. There is much of the old days in this gathering. Major Ferguson and his Tory legion threaten us with fire and sword and the hanging of our leader, which seems a great irony, for we have elected one William Campbell to be our general. That name would have brought mutiny when I was a youth. This Campbell never knew the Highlands of Scotland, for his father came to the American colonies from Ireland in 1733. Yet strange it is that I should follow a Campbell off to war. I would have thought it a mirthless jest during that balmy summer of my fourteenth year.

To that which enriches our lives with tears and laughter, memory gives a golden light, and I can see myself lying in the high heather, content in that uncommon summer heat. The sky above was a blue and bottomless well, full of lazy apple blossom clouds and wheeling larks and plovers. Far below were the stone and sod cottages of the village, their peat fires barely smoldering. I could name the owners of each one—Rankins, MacCools, Hendersons, and MacPhails, five hundred souls at most and all children of the clan.

With May's Beltane fires* we lads who kept the summer herd had driven the black cattle higher week by week into fresh pastures during the long season of the "summer dim," when the nights were full of hidden colors and the northern lights flickered in the sky. Then we herders seldom ventured down to the village but gathered at dusk close to one of the bothies, lest it rain, and frightened one another with tales of older times when every cave and rock hid cruel and crawling things, the sons and daughters of darkness. Witches, wizards, and werewolves were as real to us as the ghosts that flocked to the ringing of church bells like moths on a foggy night. Was the woman who came through the village with her barrow just an old tinker, or the terrible Bean Nighe, who washed her shroud nightly in the waters of the Coe? One or the other, we lads agreed she ought to be burned at the stake, but none of us had the courage to ask her to leave the glen.

We took turns going down to the village on ceilidh nights, when there were songs and dancing to the pipes and fiddle. My father said piping could never be too loud, and when he did not play he danced, leaping high and coming down on his toes so softly you could scarcely hear him land.

It was not all storytelling and ceilidhs for the children of the glen. There was a schoolmaster sometimes. The church kept no parish school, but a teacher was hired in, and the parents paid out fees in peat-meal-pence, as they say. For six pence a day, Mr. McPhee—he was the teacher I remember best—taught us about Rome and the Church and how to read the classics; and he was a good teacher, for we learned from him as fast as fear could teach us.

---

*See glossary (page 135) for definitions of unfamiliar terms.

Otherwise my job was to practice on the pipes when time allowed. It was all I asked for, until the rumors began. There had been talk the year before of Britain's war with France, and how King James might return to Scotland. There was much speculation in the village, and although nothing had come yet, something seemed already there. Strange thoughts played through my head when I heard such rumors, like the rumble of talking thunder or distant war pipes. We in Glencoe had little knowledge of the outside world. Were we oppressed by England? Some said so, but it was hard for me to know just how. Did we fight for the real, or for the shadow of things? Was that flapping banner, when it came, no more than a bit of colored cloth? I never asked such questions as a youth.

I had few thoughts for royalty during those summer days, and since this is my story, it is not for me to write a history of the luckless Stuarts, but my fourteenth year so much belonged to them that I cannot well get on without a few words. The Stuarts ruled in Scotland for many a lifetime, and some were good like King James I, and others bad. Queen Mary of Scotland, for example, had her head cut off, though it was her son, King James VI, who was proclaimed king of England when old Queen Elizabeth died childless.

Suffice it to say that England was never content with our Scottish kings. Yet another James, the second of England, was driven from his throne, and that summer when I was fourteen his son, calling himself James III, lived in Italy. The English called him the Old Pretender, or Old Mister Melancholy. I gather he was a dark and dour man, unfit for leading armies, but there were many Scots who wanted him back on the throne and called themselves Jacobites, after the Latin for James. James III returned to Scotland just once, in 1715, which was when my father piped and fought at Sheriffmuir. When James caught cold and took a ship back to France, few remained with heart to carry on the fight. But not long after, James had a son, who grew up with a taste for battle, as they say. I don't recall when we first began referring to that son as Bonnie Prince Charlie, but it had a romantic ring. When we heard young Prince Charles might be returning as regent to raise the Highlands against the English, most of the lads in the glen said, "Fine, let him come." What a romantic fool I was then—and must be still, to be plodding through the Carolinas with a rifle on my shoulder. Yet the name, Bonnie Prince Charlie, still has a happy ring, you can't deny it.

Rumors of French fleets scattered by storms and of the English routed from the field at Fontenoy scarcely touched me that summer in the high meadows, no more than wind in the treetops. I much preferred thinking about Peggy Sinclair and mastering the bagpipes. There seemed to be plenty of time for both.

I recall we had driven the cattle to Coire Gabhail, the Hollow of Capture, where raiders liked to hide stolen herds. Here, even in summer, the wind howled down the sky, hooing like ancient ghosts, and before the inky dark could creep up like a black tide from the glen, we had gathered the stock together there and made a fire, for with August the long cold nights were returning. In twilight all made for safe shelter before the curfew tolled in the valley, for night was made for chaos and was sanctuary to creatures who meant us only harm.

On one such afternoon of raging sunlight, with thunderheads building out to sea as clear and distinct as white paper cutouts, my father came trudging up the long slopes. I saw him first passing through the fields of barley and kale. It was a rare visit, particularly so late in the day. "What brings you here?" I hailed him. I think my voice sounded shrill,

11

for I had a feeling something not easily undone might have happened.

"Don't fuss, laddie. 'Tis just that he's finally come."

"Come?" I thought this might mean Angus Og, and perhaps Peggy as well.

"Aye, Prince Charles. Come to seek his father's crown."

That night in the hollow with the lowing cattle we forgot about ghosts and vampires and talked of ancient battles and the gathering of armies. Next day one of the lads swore he'd seen the fiery cross, or for certain a moving flame in the glen. We didn't know it then, but Prince Charlie's Year had begun. Even there on the mountainside we began to hear bits and pieces, sticking them together in the firelight: two ships bound from France, one of them routed by an English man o' war, the other guided safely to Scotland by a welcoming golden eagle, the king of birds; the prince safely ashore in the Outer Isles but told to go home by Alexander MacDonald of Boisdale, to which the prince replied, "I am come home, sir," thus shaming the chiefs with his shining courage. And so first Donald Cameron of Lochiel, and then other chiefs, one by one, agreed to share the young prince's fate.

Such talk must have stirred up the bard in my blood, for I began trying to master the old tune "When the King Enjoys His Own Again," never guessing how often I would hear it played upon the eve of battle. To be in the hills and out of touch became agony. Why did the bells ring in the church? Had someone died? It was too early for curfew. One stormy night I heard the tramp of marching feet going toward the east. There seemed to be an uneasy whisper in the air until dawn.

Then we were called down with the cattle. Since the harsh winters of 1743 and '44, we could ill afford to let the stock wander, for so many cattle had died. There was disease in some glens, and there were thieves abroad to steal those cattle that remained. I was told that my sister Mary would take my place with the herd, and I wondered if she could manage them for a day or two, never guessing it was a job that would last her a lifetime. I saw her standing beyond the herd, still as a deer listening for danger, as I hurried on alone to our cottage.

It was no great house like that of MacIain's at Carnoch, but our home had stone walls and a well-thatched roof, with three rooms below plus a loft, and we had two windows and a clay-daubed chimney, to let out the smoke, which spared us the red-rimmed eyes of the common folk.

"The MacDonalds are rising all over Scotland," my father informed me at the door. His voice was calm, but I knew he was excited. "The Chief has called us out." When a chief called, the clan obeyed, as surely as children heed a strict father, for in the old tongue *clan* means "children," and a refusal could see a man literally dragged off by his heels.

As bard and piper, my father's only choice was loyalty. A favorite saying of his was, "When an Englishman spits in your face, do you say, 'Oh, I knew it would rain'?" Once he set his teeth into something my father left them there. The restoration of the Stuart kings was such a cause with him, and he was proud that the old cause was alive and that there were still men willing to die for Scotland.

The only real issue had to do with me, for my mother was saying, "Oh, no, absolutely. The lad's too young."

"Och, what a carry on." My father softly jangled some coins in his sporran. "In the old days . . ."

"No more 'old days' out of you," she interrupted. My father and mother enjoyed stormy arguments, slammed doors, jutting jaws.

"We'll be needing every man and boy," my father went on. His voice was hearty and coaxing. I stood quietly. It

13

was not the time for me to talk, as my father paced back and forth, ignoring the tension. Playfully he squeezed my shoulder. "When this lad was born I said, 'Here's one for freedom.' Who dares say no to fighting for freedom?" It sounded so simple and bold, while the craven alternative was being bound and chained, with which I had no experience at the time.

"You're far too old for such foolish talk," my mother argued, "and Colin's too young. That prince of yours will bring only sorrow and trouble, mark my words. The Stuarts are born to sorrow and trouble."

She was right again. Everyone said my mother had the second sight, which no one ever heeded. My father was determined, and so was I. The argument never really came to an end. Father just went out to dig up the old weapons hidden since the Disarming Act.

I remember my mother sat down and looked silently out the window, defeated. Then my sister Mary came in quietly and told me the herd was safely locked away in the pen. Without Mary there would have been no question of my leaving, for I would have been left behind to care for the black cattle, as were many lads, for cattle meant life to a Highlander. Mary might have said no. I wonder sometimes how different it might have been, but she said no word of complaint. I do recall her glancing at our mother and then back at me, and saying something strange. "But look ye, Colin, the wolf begins to prowl."

"You're daft," I said. There had been no wolves in years.

"Aye," said Mary, "he snuffles on the path. He pushes at the gate."

I did hear something, and the hair on the back of my neck began to prickle. Then I heard Father's voice. "Och," I told her, " 'tis only Father," and she turned and looked at me over her shoulder and said, "Did I say it was not?"

Father came in with Grandfather's sword with its silver basket, the one he'd carried at Killiecrankie. The original blade had broken on the shoulder of a fleeing lobsterback. Its replacement was engraved with the words "Prosperity to Scotland and No Union," which is another way of saying no to England.

"Here it is," Father said, glaring at me fiercely, and I thought with a shudder, Good Lord, what a proud old man. He rubbed a cloth down the blade, which was like a slender beam of blue-gray light in the fire's glow, and I realize now I was transfixed by the romance of it all.

Mother sat with the flat of her hand pressed against her cheek as though she had an awful toothache, then she rose and said, "If you go wagging that sword around here, I'll have to put it in a safe place away from bairns who don't know better."

That much was done for my mother, and for a few days the sword was laid aside, but the royal standard was to be raised at Glenfinnan on the nineteenth of August, which meant the MacDonalds of Glencoe would set out at dawn on the sixteenth.

The day before, Mary left quietly for the high pastures. Uncomplaining, she gave me a hug and told me to be careful.

"I'll be careful," I promised her, and during the fighting thereafter, when I saw the smoke curling up from the lines of lobsterbacks and the flash of their bayonets, I thought of our solemn exchange and could not help faintly smiling.

"And take my love to Angus Og." I promised this also. Then she was gone with the black cattle.

I remember the dawn coming the next morning, my last at home. It began with gray, a vast grayness in the air, which emptied the world of mountains and valleys. I could hear cattle coughing somewhere in the mist, and I thought for a moment that Mary had returned to betray me.

Father and I dressed silently, until Mother said, "It's easier for a man to clothe himself for war than a woman for parting." Her eyes impressed some hidden significance into mine, and then she threw her big red arms about my neck and kissed my cheek so hard I nearly lost my balance. Father had buckled on the old sword. A dirk in its dark leather sheath hung from his belt. He'd cradled the pipes as well, so we stepped off in style. For a weapon I had only a herder's staff, to help with the stock on the march. The end of the staff was fitted with a kind of makeshift Lochaber ax fashioned from a scythe.

Fifty MacDonalds marched out of the Glen that morning. The rest of the men pledged to follow once they'd brought in the harvest. We marched behind our chief and the skirling pipes, heading west to Loch Linnhe. For many it was the high road which meant no returning.

We planned to cross Loch Linnhe by boat, not wanting to encounter the government garrison at Fort William, with its long-range guns. Angus Og and the Sinclairs would help us there, we hoped. Most were Jacobite in spirit, but their chief had declined to lead them out. He'd gone soft, they said. Angus Og explained that on a winter raid into Campbell country they had spent the night in a high corrie full of snow, and the chief had rolled up a white ball to put under his head. Angus Og concluded with his easy smile, "A man who can't bide the night without a pillow is a lassie inside." Angus Og did not look like a fighter, with his handsome, always cheerful face, but when the drums beat he was never found wanting.

Had not the Campbells sided with the English, no Sinclair would have rallied. The same was true of the MacLeans

16

of Mull and the Camerons of Lochiel. Hatred of the Campbells had much to do with our clan turning out to a man, and a good many others as well. No question, the Highlands were much divided where the Stuart cause was concerned, though I didn't know it then and would not have cared, being a soldier with the important business of saying goodbye to his sweetheart.

Peggy Sinclair, you were in blossom that summer. People say that of young girls, and with my Peggy it was just right. But she was more than pretty. She had a neat firm chin and lips some might call too large, but they fit firmly together. In moments of pleasure, she had the face of a child, but when she was serious you could see the woman she was going to be, so determined and fearless it was startling.

We took our leave on the rocky lochside. There was no privacy, but she gave me a kiss on the lips and was standing back before I could detain her. "Nothing is going to happen to you," she said, with what seemed reassuring confidence.

"No fear, I'll be back," I told her. Then it was clambering into the boat and waving. Her curly hair blew across her smiling mouth. This was the great adventure, I told myself. From this day on I would be a man, and yet a small boy crouched deep inside me and was afraid.

The boat pulled away into the shimmering, blue-black, fathomless loch. Mist hung like ice in shreds above the surface. At first the wet oars winked us along until the clouds closed overhead. Soon it would rain. We hunched over the oars, and presently the rain began to fall.

# 3

From the lochside to Glenfinnan was not so far as I had reckoned, but it was all adventure—seeing the world, tossing aside the smells of home, swinging our shoulders with a looselimbed stride. I was new to marching then. We arrived above the loch toward evening on the second day, with time taken along the way for hunting. One hundred and ten MacDonalds and Sinclairs, counting lads like myself and a few women, we all expected to see a great host gathered below, as they tell of in the Bible.

"Look ye, yon's Loch Shiel," said Angus Og. We stopped among wispy pines, peering down over rocky slopes streaked black and shiny with falling streams. Dark clouds like another range of mountains rose beyond the loch, which was long and empty and glowed like polished pewter. The only sound was the wind and the small waves lapping the shore. Not a soul was in sight.

We camped where we stood for fear of entrapment below. The hunting parties had killed a deer, which we ate raw after pressing the meat between two boards to force out the blood, for we were ordered not to build fires. The loch lay calm and the clouds parted once to reveal the sky as thick with stars as a deep pool of silver minnows. I wrapped my plaid about me and slept.

There was a smell and feel of dawn long before the east began to glow, though I'd heard men stirring in their half sleep. I had never before been in the midst of such a crowd, but I'd never felt so lost and lonely alone in the hills with the cattle.

When I saw my father moving, I whispered, "Will any more be coming?"

"Aye, with the morn," he replied, and rolled over.

The morning brought mist boiling down from the mountains to lie like snow on the mirror-still loch. Still no one came. There was talk of going home, and criticism of the prince. "I heard Charlie's teachers didna' think he was very bright," Angus Og said cheerfully, but he was never enthusiastic about the Stuarts. Father insisted Prince Charles was a bold rider and a fine shot, just the sort to win back a lost throne.

It wasn't my place to say, "Too bad, time to go home," but I think many of us were beginning to think that way, when the heavy slabs of mist began to heave away from the mountainsides. Light slipped through, with a great shaft knifing down upon the water to reveal three boats skimming our way. Just three small boats, carrying no more than threescore men, and yet somehow we knew. In the spreading sunshine, the first tall figure stepped ashore. It was a moment I'll not forget. The prince had come to us, and despite his somber abbot's robe, it was like seeing the idea of royalty, startling in the flesh-and-blood fact of his being there. I had no words at the time. He might have been a demigod, at the very least one of those rare creatures Destiny has set upon the earth to serve its own purpose. Of course, all this was before I got to know him.

Only a handful of farmers met the prince when he strode ashore at Glenfinnan, and when the rain began again he retired to one of their huts before I got there. Curtains of

19

rain drifted down the loch and we huddled by the shore, wondering what was wrong, until in early afternoon someone pointed out movement on the upper slopes, seen, then lost in the rain, seen again and growing until we knew. Believe me, when the last of us are long gone and forgotten, there will be someone to say, "If I'd only heard them piping, if I'd only seen them marching there." Two columns worked their way down the mountain trail, eight hundred Camerons of Lochiel, four hundred MacDonalds of Keppoch, with fifty redcoat prisoners taken a few days before at Spean Bridge as the Highlanders were hurrying south from Lochaber.

I mention Keppoch particularly, for we MacDonalds of Glencoe, as the smallest branch of the great Clan Donald, were joined to them in the campaign to come. Good men they were, and it was MacDonald of Keppoch who, when told by a guest of the great candelabras he'd seen in fine English homes, had ringed his dining table around with clansmen, each bearing a flaming pine knot. "Who in England has such candlesticks?" Keppoch had then asked his guest.

There would be no fleeing from the English by such men, and when they had all filed down to the lochside, the prince, clad now as a Highlander, emerged from his hut. Then, as we all stood about, a dottery old man who seemed scarcely able to walk was helped to an earthen mound. We gathered around him, for this, I was told, was the marquess of Tullibardine, the true duke of Atholl, though the government had bestowed the title upon his traitorous younger brother. With assistance, Tullibardine unfurled the red-and-white flag of King James III, father of our Prince Charles, which Bishop Hugh MacDonald of Morar proceeded to bless in this holy cause. A great cheer went up, echoing through the lonely glen. We were at war! Another

20

shout rose for the unfurling of the red-and-gold Scottish lion, for which so many MacDonalds had fallen at Bannockburn and Flodden.

No more was necessary, but Tullibardine dragged things out, delivering a long speech in a quavering voice full of scattered pauses and throat clearings. Then the prince spoke, about glory and loyalty and delivering Scotland from misery and oppression, though I couldn't understand what he could do about the winter cold and the dying cattle, which was our biggest problem, as I saw it. The fact is that Prince Charles, having been raised in Italy, was not that easy to understand, and his mixture of Scots and English had a strange accent to our ears. I also think, perhaps, his tongue was a wee bit too long, for he seemed to lisp in any language. But who needed to understand every word? We all knew what he meant, and when he struggled to give the king's health in Gaelic, *Deoch Slaint an Rich,* the greatest shout of all went up. Men and boys, if the path the prince chose led to Hell, all of us would have followed then.

But we went nowhere that day or the next. Despite the intermittent rain, these were exuberant hours spent at Glenfinnan. To a youth accustomed to herding cattle in a lonely glen it seemed a mighty host indeed, and I would have been shocked if anyone had pointed out what an ill-armed and poorly shod rabble we were. The only soldiers there were Keppoch, who'd served the French, and John William O'Sullivan, the prince's Irish companion, who as adjutant general tried to form us up into companies of fifty men each. It did not work, for a Highlander fights with his clan or not at all, but then O'Sullivan never did comprehend our Highland ways. I don't believe he ever could tell one clan from another, supposing there might be a family pattern in the tartans we wore. There wasn't, of course. Some wore the great belted plaids, and some the new phillibeg or short plaid, which was easier for getting about but didn't give the same protection at night.

In fact, the old belted plaid was so long and heavy most men cast it aside before charging into battle, which meant that if you didn't fancy going home naked you could ill afford to lose. A very few, mostly the highborn, wore trews. Weapons of any sort were in short supply. I still had my makeshift ax and others carried scythes and the like, but the well-equipped men had a dirk and pistols in their belts and a broadsword at their sides, and targets on their left arm to ward off sword blades—and bullets too, with luck. Almost all of us wore a bonnet of some sort, which was where each clan displayed its traditional badge. Ours was a sprig of heather. The MacNeils, who came from the Western Isles, favored a bit of seaweed, and for the Stuarts all of us wore the white cockade as well.

We camped out that night and the next, as we would until the snow fell, and the place was a dark forest of glowworm light, mysterious voices, laughter, and song, for only after an easy victory is an army as exuberant as an army newly formed that has not fought at all.

The last morning the prince rode around camp on a white charger, a fine horse Keppoch had taken from the English. With some sunlight finding its way down through the heavy clouds, Charlie looked very bright and fine—come into his hour, as they say—but by the time we marched the sky had closed over again and birds were flying low. No time to begin a journey. Still, off we went with Charlie now on foot, striding up and down the line of men, shouting with laughter and slapping us on our shoulders.

I'd wager we were fifteen hundred strong at the time, counting the boys and women, but rumors came back that the prince had raised thirty thousand—the army we might have had if every fighting man in the Highlands had been there. Not once did we approach that many, not even in victory; but the prince had said he would never look back to see if a single man was following him. I believe he meant that, for, though some said later that Charlie was a coward, I cannot accept that. With all his faults, Charles Edward Stuart was a brave man.

"He's a royal terror, that's what he is," my father complained with admiration for the way the prince could walk. He nearly marched the lot of us into the ground. Of course, he wore good Italian shoes while most of us were barefoot or shod in thin brogues and unaccustomed to the hard gravel roads General Wade had cut into the Highlands. Then, too, there was the rain. No stranger to Scotland, it never seemed to let up. Curtains of it like glass beads swayed in the wind, rattling down so thick herring might have swum through the air. That first night I was so tired I didn't really mind the wet; I just lay down on the pine needles and slept. Nothing seemed to matter.

The next morning we came to a river ford and a fork in the road. Between steep banks of meadowsweet we slid about on slippery stones while clouds of gnats swarmed around us. Just beyond the road forked, right to Loch Linnhe and home, left to the north and the high pass at Corrieyairack. If I hesitated, it was only for a moment. Then, with the others, I trudged north toward the pass, where rumor had it that General Sir John Cope had assembled all the government troops in Scotland, two redcoats for every one of us.

# 4

*Sycamore Shoals*
SEPTEMBER 24, 1780

A sudden wind has sprung up, a rain wind smelling of the deep forests here in North Carolina. These forests are deeper than those I knew as a youth in Scotland, yet the scent excites memories of how it was to feel young and adventurous.

Along the shores of Loch Eil we marched on that long-ago day, avoiding the guns of Fort William, and on to Lochgarry Castle by way of the mountain road. The prince had twenty-five field cannon in tow, but the terrain was hard and we Highlanders have always scorned menial tasks like hauling guns. So the cannon were abandoned beside the road, and perhaps it was just to punish us for our laziness that the prince tramped on for sixteen miles.

When one of Charlie's boots threw its heel, there were some of us who prayed for a painful blister, but he didn't slacken his pace, though it cut him down a bit from six feet, which left him still a head taller than most of us. We Highlanders were small for the most part, but my children are larger than their mother or myself at that age, no doubt thanks to the bounty of food this new land produces for our benefit. But back to my own stunted fourteenth year. We were tired, and hungry, and mildewed with the rain. Faces glared out of sodden plaids, bleak and cold. I don't know what my fellow clansmen would have done to the Red Coats just then, but they looked a fierce and frightening lot to me.

Then I began thinking about the government army up ahead, groping for us as we were looking for them. War seemed an odd business, now that I considered it. The men around me did not look nervous, but were they ready to meet the dragon and slay him or were they quietly quaking with fear and ready to turn and flee at the first alarm? Of course, when I wondered about the others, I was really wondering about myself.

General Cope was said to be waiting at Corrieyairack. "A hard place to take," said Angus Og, who knew the pass well. By now my nose had begun to itch, a clear sign that danger was near at hand. We'd be in it soon, and of course we'd win. But moment by moment, how would it be? I'd killed some rabbits and geese, but I'd never seen a person die, except at home and in bed. What with my father's songs and stories I'd heard battle cries and the clang of steel down the ages, since the campaigns of Achilles and Hector. In ballads the air was full of flying legs, arms, and heads, but they were always the legs, arms, and heads of villains. Mind you, I was not so innocent to suppose that, as in the ballads, the enemy always lost. I only knew that we could not afford to lose. With equal certainty, I knew that neither Father nor Angus Og would ever turn and flee the field. I pictured them as the berserks of old, gnashing their shields with that battle rage of which the bards so often sing. If they stood their ground to the last, then so must I. There grew the nagging doubt that if I had any courage at all, it was just a kind of shame at being afraid.

At Lochgarry Castle the word went around that General Cope and nearly four thousand men had just left Fort William for the pass at Corrieyairack, and that he meant to fire down upon us with swivel guns. We marched to meet him there as shafts of rain joined sky to mountain, and we could make out few of the seventeen traverses that comprised the pass—so many opportunities for an ambush. My pulse began to beat in my ears like a distant drum: *dum de dum, dum de dum.*

With scouts gone ahead, we waited, while I raged inside at the doubts that had begun to gnaw away at a lifetime's conviction that death was for other people. God had simply made me different in that respect. And on that occasion my vanity held, for I did not die at Corrieyairack. None of us did. We marched right up and through the pass, once the word came that General Cope was heading north as well. Was Cope a fool, or only pretending to be? The prince toasted his chiefs in brandy, declaring, "To the health of Mr. Cope, and may every general in the usurper's service prove himself as much a friend as he has done."

In truth, most of us were disappointed. I was, but I slept well that night and never intended to admit the great relief I felt inside, not even to Father. Then all of a sudden, Angus Og found me out. It went like this. I was just sitting there after the day's march, staring at the rain, when he came over and asked, "What's the matter, Colin? Rain getting ye down?"

"Just thinking," I replied.

"And a heavy thought to hold with both hands," he said. "Were ye feared this morning?" Then out it came. I found myself nodding in assent. "Will ye harken to that, now. The lad was trembling in his brogues and didna' say a word. Well, that's naught so bad, Colin. No, I esteem ye none the less. Dinna think only bairns and lassies are afeared. Go tell anyone, Angus Og Sinclair was scared stiff this day, and will be again. Only a fool would be otherwise."

"How do you think I'll do when the time comes?" I asked him.

"Och, you'll do just fine in a fight. You've as stout a heart as any man." I think I must have stared at him in a confusion of gratitude and love. "Get away with you, Colin. You'll do just fine."

That night I found myself singing, and it was not a brave attempt to hide my homesickness and fear but a selfish desire to sing. Next morning early we were on the march again, hot on Cope's trail, I supposed. With the English—the Sassenach, we called them—on the run, an easy victory was expected, with plunder to follow, and plunder was a magical word that kept many a greedy Highlander in the field, though it shames me to admit it.

We marched every day, all day, with the crags breaking down and the hills beginning to roll. Although the prince had a groom and a cook and lodged well at night, he marched on foot with us every step of the way, first with one clan and then with another. There were very few stragglers at this time, not even the women, who often bore heavy loads of laundry or fuel for the evening's fire. The women had to be careful not to cross the road ahead of the column of men, particularly in bare feet, for that was an evil omen. On the other hand, meeting an armed man was said to be a good portent, and we met many such who chose to join us.

Each morning we started out with a steady swish and chime of metal on metal, an undertone of voices and jests becoming complaints, and finally silence. By afternoon a few limped or sat beside the road examining their feet, hoping, I suppose, to rejoin their clans by evening. Father

27

cautioned me more than once: "You don't need a brain to be a soldier; only a strong arm to strike with and feet to keep moving. If your feet give out, laddie, you're done, so be kind to them."

Thanks to chasing cattle around the hillsides I had tough feet. It was sleep I needed, and I seemed scarcely to have lain down at night when Angus Og was pressing my arm and whispering, "Come on, Colin, let's go. If this be the road to Hell, at least it's all downhill."

It was at the foot of these hills that a council of war was held. They decided to let General Cope go his way, which seemed to mean Inverness and the sea. Never interrupt your enemy when he's making a mistake, we were told. There was grumbling over the loss of spoils, and then Angus Og said it might be a temptation to march on the now unguarded Lowlands and Edinburgh; but was it wise to leave an undefeated enemy in the north who might well be reinforced by sea?

In any case we headed east and south through Perthshire toward Blair Atholl. This was the marquess of Tullibardine's ancestral home, and many of his tenant farmers flocked out to greet us. This helped our spirits, as did the weather, for a gusty wind had swept away the clouds. Sheets of blue, white, and gray let down blades of silver and gold. For the first time since I had left home no rain fell in the night, and I awoke to see drops of dew had settled on the sleeping men and traced their bodies in pearls. Tall grass brushed my ankles like strokes of limber icicles, but otherwise, for the first time in days, my body was dry.

While we marched through the region of Badenoch the prince was with us, asking about our families and our songs and legends, and I thought Charlie was as fine as a prince could be.

That night or the next—I have trouble remembering—

we camped at Dalwhinnie on the open moor next to Ruthven Barracks, where a small government garrison held out. They were no threat to us, so we ignored them and fished for salmon in the River Garry while the women washed clothing downstream, their coats tucked up and their bare legs red as blood in the cold water. They stamped about in sudsy tubs with their arms thrown around each other's shoulders for support, and I could not help but smile, imagining Peggy laughing among them, and Mother and Mary, too. I missed them all.

By now the sun had returned entirely, and for the first time in weeks the sky was truly blue. The heather was purple. Cornflowers, lady's slippers, and gorse flowered yellow as egg yolks. It was good to be alive, and I remember Angus Og throwing a kiss to the breeze and shouting, "Aye, Scotland!"

Presently we tramped down a long avenue of lime trees, the Jacobite host armed with swords and muskets from half a dozen countries and as many forgotten wars. Behind us on a pony cart trundled the artillery, one small, unmounted brass cannon. Up ahead rose the walls and turrets of Blair Castle. James Murray, duke of Atholl and a government man, had fled, leaving it to his older brother, the marquess of Tullibardine. Blair Castle was the first touch of civilization the prince had seen since reaching Scotland. Hohum to a prince raised in Rome and Paris, but it seemed very grand to me.

On the last day of August Charlie reviewed us there at Blair. The thinness of our ranks came as a shock, since a good many had wandered home once Cope had gotten away. Angus Og shook his head, blaming the prince for letting Cope escape. "Never count on a redhead," he said. "The stock of Cain, you know." I have to admit that sometimes the prince's ways puzzled me. Here we were in the middle of a desperate war, with foes to north and south, and the prince with a bounty of thirty thousand pounds sterling on his head, and he decides to take a few days off to go hunting. Not hunting for food, for the hunger would not come until later, but hunting for sport. I could only suppose that was how royalty did things; and besides, I welcomed the rest, and the early autumn weather was grand.

Our last hope of turning on General Cope vanished as we marched due south from Blair Castle, and with the Highlands melting away behind us there was more grumbling. At Lude, the seat of Clan Robertson, a ball was held in honor of Prince Charles, and if we cared to we could peer through the windows and see him gliding about. His long legs seemed to be elegantly suited to dancing.

On September the third we marched through Dunkeld with no opposition. You could see forty miles in the clear autumn air. Back home the first leaves must have been drifting down, and soon snow would come to lie silent under the deep green of pine and spruce. It seemed late in the year to be going off to war.

Prince Charles rode ahead on his white horse into Perth to have his father proclaimed king at the market cross. I recall he wore a suit of tartan trimmed in gold lace, and a big crowd turned out, as the harvest fair was being held there at the time. We must have looked a fierce and barbarous crew to what appeared to our eyes to be Lowland folk, though we had not yet crossed the Highland line.

For a week we camped at the King's Park in Perth while the clans came in to join up. Viscount Strathallan, Lord Ogilvie, John Roy Stuart, the laird of Gask and Aldie, Robertson of Struan, Blairfitty, and Cushevale led in their children. Some were eager to fight, and others downcast. We wished them all good fortune: "May your chiefs have the ascendancy." Within that week the ranks swelled to three thousand strong, though a third of these were discounted as useless when it came to a fight. Not knowing where I stood myself, I made fun of no one.

I should say a word now about Lord George Murray, for he became nearly as important as the prince himself in the months to follow. I think we never had a tougher or more gifted soldier. Father knew him from the "Fifteen" when he fought at Sheriffmuir and he was out again four years later at Glenshiel. There were some who didn't like his blunt and overbearing manner, but Murray had a talent for war and was the sort who slept on the ground wrapped in his plaid with his men. I heard him once tell the chiefs, "I do not ask you, my lords, to go before, but merely to follow me." Yet I think there was humanity in the man, and I believe the tears of widows and orphans were his tears as well. I know he left a beloved family at home and came to the prince's cause reluctantly, but he believed passionately that the Stuarts had been falsely deprived of their crown. I do not feel that the romantic appeal that bound so many of us to the prince at first ever really touched Murray. He simply tried to do his best to right an old wrong and win back the crown, though I now suspect he felt the cause was doomed.

Lord George and the prince were very different men—too different, perhaps. While Murray studied the battle-field and measured the size of the regiments on either side, Charlie saw only the shining goal to which he believed God's good will would carry him. Charlie imagined himself a kind of miracle worker, and we simple Highlanders agreed. He was a bit of a miracle—he had to be—who never counted the cost. George Murray always had a good idea what the cost in lives must be for doing this or that, and only if the move was worth that price would he make

31

it. For this some hot-tempered men called him traitor, which I'll vouch he never was, while others claim he was a defeatist from the first. Who knows? That might be. There is a saying: "Had Prince Charles slept during all of Charlie's Year," allowing Murray to act for him according to his own judgment, "the prince would have found the British crown upon his head when he awoke." For myself I doubt this, but the great ifs of history I leave to scholars. I know what happened to me and how I saw it, and I say here only that a cause is ill favored when a prince and his general cannot see eye to eye.

Before leaving Perth we shuffled through a review. I thought it quite fine, not yet having seen redcoats filing into battle, and Charlie was delighted, calling us, "My stags!" Lord George Murray directed the distribution of meal sacks so we would not scavenge the Lowland farms as the hordes of old had done. After all, we came to them as liberators.

On the eleventh day of September we left Perth and crossed the Firth of Forth at the Queen's Ferry. We arrived at Dunblane, not far from where Father had fought in the "Fifteen." Here some MacGregors of Glencairnaig came in, along with the rest of our MacDonalds. All was well in Glencoe, they assured us. There was a letter from Mother, telling me to be careful and eat sensibly. Angus Og had a letter from Mary, saying if I stayed away much longer she'd have the cattle under such control I might as well stay away for good. Peggy had enclosed a note, which made me smile and want to cry at the same time.

Presently we marched on to the Ford of Frew, not far from Doune, where they make the fine pistols. Three young ladies named Edmonstone came out giggling to offer wine to the prince, and then they waved and waved as we went by. They were pretty, and we waved back. I suppose they are still there, matrons now, living along the only road they ever knew. For many of us in the ranks swaying by, it was the last of all roads; and for all of us, laughing and waving there, it was a mystery, this road to war.

At Frew we entered the Lowlands, and Father shouldered his pipes and said it was like Caesar crossing the Rubicon. Up and down the line other pipers began to play, and Prince Charles drew his sword and held it high as he mounted the far bank of the river.

The pipes were playing as we passed beneath Stirling Castle on its high hill. This must have provoked the government garrison within, for they fired cannon at us without doing any harm. We just marched on, pretending to ignore the guns, until we were out of range. "Keep out of the way of cannonballs," Father cautioned, "even when they are spent. They'll do more damage than you think." Obvious advice, but later Father made the mistake of forgetting his own words.

We camped in the famous meadow of Bannockburn within sight of Stirling Castle. This was our first Lowland camp, and it built up our spirits to be on such hallowed ground where Scotland had won her greatest victory. Over four hundred years had passed since Robert the Bruce defeated the English in 1314 and won back the crown of Scotland, which more often than not sat on an English head. I am boasting in telling this story, for the MacDonalds fought so well at Bannockburn that ever after we were granted the honor of holding the right flank of the royal army. Rest assured that many a MacDonald bard kept this privilege alive in song and story. The sad irony is that it provided one more nail for the Jacobite coffin before Prince Charlie's Year was done.

At Bannockburn we faced a choice: Edinburgh or Glasgow, Scotland's two great Lowland cities. Glasgow was rich and unprotected and had no use for Jacobites. Edinburgh had a fearful castle full of government troops; yet it was the capital.

Edinburgh sets a kind of tidal pull upon all Highlanders, and we sensed it before the order to march came down. Lord George Murray saw to it that our meal bags were full, and we were warned that looters would be severely punished. I heard later that a man caught stealing a sheep was shot dead by young Lochiel.

Gray autumn clouds were piling up above the western mountains and crowding into the valleys as we swung away from Bannockburn. We halted the night of the fourteenth of September near Falkirk. The place meant nothing to me at the time, but it was destined to be the site of my first battle—that is, the first battle in which I truly fought. Even then we were half expecting a fight, for government dragoons had been watching us and we were told they might try and hold the bridge at Linlithgow.

As we formed up to march from Falkirk, a sharp rumbling was heard. Heads came up and a few hands reached for swords. Then Angus Og laughed. " 'Tis the good Lord's artillery." Thunder rumbled, and I saw a greenish flutter of lightning, but no rain fell. I now think of it as a presentiment.

As we marched on Linlithgow the dragoons fled before us. It was a Sunday, September 15, but worship was suspended as we marched through town. People lined the road with their Sabbath dignity intact, neither hostile nor sad, to see us pass. We halted four miles eastward, with the Firth of Forth widening into the gray-blue sea on our left. Where we camped there was a milestone that marked twelve miles to Edinburgh.

Like Stirling, Edinburgh is a place you can see from miles away—particularly the castle, which holds the high ground.

As with Stirling, the castle was firmly in government hands, and the great gates of the city were barred to us. The big difference was that no one expected we would just march by as we had at Stirling.

As we trudged toward Edinburgh, the city seemed the key to everything—the key to Scotland, the key to the Stuart crown. Win Edinburgh and we would win all; fail and we would lose the war. I had little doubt we would take the city—at a price. It all seemed within reach that September morning in 1745. With luck, the gates would swing open and bells would ring in welcome. One way or another, once Edinburgh fell we would have done our duty and everyone could go home before winter set in, with a few new tales to tell beside the fire.

# 5

Believe me, there is nothing here in the Carolinas to compare with that first distant view of Edinburgh, with the castle rising from its crag and the spear points of kirk steeples stabbing at the sky. "Yon's the capital," Father said. "You can smell it from here." He had visited Edinburgh before and had no love of the place, though I thought it a grand sight to behold and still do. However, 'tis a harsh and stony city where they burned men and women for witchcraft not long ago and shed not a tear.

It was rumored the city was in turmoil, with the town guard feeling old and the trained bands not knowing whether to fight or flee. It was said they were being urged to hold the walls against us, the Highland savages, until General Cope could come for their deliverance from the north, and the city gates remained fast shut against us.

There was talk of a siege, but we were ill equipped to mount one. "It's naught so hard," Angus Og argued. "Yon walls are only fit for keeping out smugglers. One rush and we'd be in. That's the way of it." To try to lift our fighting spirits, the Reverend Doak preached a sermon on righteous wrath and told us our battle cry should be "The sword of the Lord and of Gideon"; but each clan had its own cry, and we would use them when the time came.

My mouth was dry with thoughts of the coming slaughter, when the provost of Edinburgh sent out a hackney coach full of deputies to negotiate with Prince Charles. "Delaying tactics," Father observed, "to give General Cope more time to get here. Come the morn, we'll be cutting at the walls." But when the provost's deputation rolled back into the city, Lochiel, dressed in riding coat and hunting cape, rode after them with a group of his own men. We heard later they were mistaken for royal dragoons, so that when the provost's coach returned through the Netherbow Gate on its way to the stables, Lochiel and his men burst in. And so, Edinburgh City was taken without a drop of blood being shed.

"Now that's the way to fight a war." Angus Og laughed, but Father said, "We'll no be so lucky again."

However, Edinburgh Castle remained in government hands, and the garrison there had no intention of surrendering. We heard that the militia had either run off or back into the castle. We took a byroad to avoid the castle's cannon and camped that night at Gray's Park. The grounds were full of ripe peas, which we ate or trampled, but to show what a civilized and public-spirited army we were, the duke of Perth gave the owner a note for payment in full.

Noon of the next day found us in Hunter's Bog, with the crags of Arthur's Seat rising up on one side and Salisbury Crags on the other. Edinburgh Castle still flew its British flag, but there was no way they could stop us from marching on Holyrood Palace a mile or so away, where the whole city seemed to have turned out to welcome Prince Charles.

37

Charlie rode ahead with the duke of Perth and Lord Elcho, and the crowd struggled forward to try to kiss his hands. It looked like the whole of the city was there, from fine ladies in their best silk tartans to dirty little street scamps with no more than a bit of blanket to cover their sooty nakedness.

Charlie had never looked more regal—tall, serious, and dignified. He rode with his left hand on the silver hilt of his sword, showing off his long slender fingers. If you kept an eye on Charlie you realized he liked to show off his hands—and everything else that day, from green velvet bonnet to blue, gold-trimmed sash and red velvet breeches and shiny black riding boots. His jacket was tartan in the Highland manner, but he looked very much the royal presence.

The crowd milled and pushed, so that James Hepburn of Keith unsheathed his sword and held it high to clear a path for the prince. Charlie pulled at his own sword, but the blade wouldn't come out of the scabbard. Then he dismounted, paused for a few more hand kisses, and disappeared into Holyrood Palace. The restive crowd cheered when he reappeared on a balcony and then began to sing "When the King Enjoys His Own Again." In all of Prince Charlie's Year there was no more glorious day than this, unless it was the one to follow.

The garrison inside Edinburgh Castle had agreed not to fire on us if they were left alone, so we marched up the city's High Street the next morning. The houses there are all of stone that is blackened from the sooty air, and up to ten stories high. Too many people crammed together behind those heavy iron-studded doors, if you ask me. A few houses of the nobility had walled gardens, downhill near Holyrood Palace, but otherwise the narrow alleys were piled high with filth and more garbage and slops pouring down day and night. It was worth your life to walk there, and even in September coal smoke belched from the gabled rooftops, so you were lucky to glimpse the blue sky. As Father had said, it smelled to high Heaven.

I would not have stopped there but for the crowning of Charlie's father, King James, at the Market Cross. The prince, all a-glitter, more than made up for his father's absence, and the crowd did its best to match him, especially the ladies. White handkerchiefs fluttered in greeting from every window of those tall dark houses. A Mrs. Murray of Broughton, sword in hand and all decorated with white ribbons in honor of the Stuarts, sat a fine white horse. Bagpipes reverberated off the stone walls and trumpets blared as James III was proclaimed king of Scotland. Then the heralds read out the royal decree for all to hear: "By virtue and authority of the above Commission of Regency granted unto us by the king, our royal father, we are now come to execute His Majesty's will and pleasure, by setting up his royal standard, and asserting his undoubted right to the throne of his ancestors . . ." and on and on.

It seemed like victory and the end of the war to me. I kept forgetting that the Stuarts expected to take back England and Ireland as well as Scotland; and even had they not such ambitions, there were silent, stern-faced Hanoverians in the crowd with an eye to the weathercocks. They did well to look, for the wind had changed and we had scarcely settled down in camp that night when the rumor spread that General Cope's fleet had been spotted in the Firth of Forth, heading for Dunbar.

Our camp was outside the city walls at Duddingston. I was glad of that, finding Edinburgh a grand place to see but no place for a Highlander raised on fresh air to stay. I'm not suggesting we were all perfume and roses—far from it—but there's a difference, and I was getting used to the aroma of an unwashed army.

At Duddingston, Lord George Murray kept us drilling all day long. We needed the training and were told it helped give the impression we were a larger army than we were in truth. Aside from the drilling, we were comfortable and ate well. Chickens were six pence a bird and ducks eight pence. A gallon of ale could be had for one shilling and four pence.

Some of our men's relatives turned up to see how the army was doing, and I wished Peggy were among them so I might say something fond and foolish into her ear. However, the only word from home was a letter for Angus Og. He read it to himself and then sauntered over and looked very sternly at me.

"There's a note from Peg," he told me, and then he very solemnly winked. "She says I'm to give you a hug for her. Do you fancy that, laddie? I'm supposed to keep you out of trouble, too." My sister Mary had suggested the reverse—that I look after Angus Og. Such directives led to a kind of agreement between us.

"No harm will come to you, Colin, if I can help it," Angus Og pledged. "Not while I'm alive." In that dark face his eyes were never more fierce.

"Aye," I swore, "and I'll do the same for you always," knowing I had the best of the bargain.

"Then smile, Colin," Angus Og said, and gleamed his teeth at me. "You can smile, can you not? Good."

I must have produced a mildewed grin resembling a happy drunk, but the moment seemed a serious one to me and still does. Right up to the last minute I kept my part of the bargain, but it is that last minute I shall forever regret.

"Och, away you go, Colin. Let's get a fire going and have some hot food."

I wasn't about to argue with that, for it had been a long

40

day, beginning with the rumor there was to be a grand assault on the castle—which was called off when the government garrison threatened to bombard the city—followed by the endless drilling, and the final news that General Cope had landed his army at Dunbar and was beginning his march to relieve Edinburgh.

Clearly the war was far from over, and I found myself yearning for a sword. The city arsenal had been seized and its contents were being handed out, but only to older men. It seemed unfair. After all, I'd been part of the Highland army since the beginning.

"You'll have no need of a sword in the rear rank," Father told me, always practical. "If need be, run away."

Both Father and Angus Og were armed with broadswords, dirks, and targets, and they shared a single musket. A few of the front rankers, usually officers, carried a brace of pistols as well. So many weapons, and me with naught but a scythe blade fit for cutting grass.

"I'm a MacDonald," I told Father, implying that a MacDonald who turned his back on the foe could never live down the disgrace.

He answered me slowly, hands behind his back and his eyes fixed on the ground. "Och, running's not so bad; not for a lad. I'll esteem you none the less." He paused thoughtfully. "But you've marched along like a soldier. You have that, Colin. I've been proud to see it." Another pause. "So look ye, it's been in the family a long while and stood witness to many a sacred oath and pledge."

I put out my hands and was barely able to whisper, "Mine?"

Then Father moved his eyelids, which was the only way he ever smiled. "Mind, it's sharp." He handed me the old family dirk, its wooden hilt shiny black with use and its long blade nearly as dark. My grandfather had carried it

41

behind his target at Killiecrankie, and it had been in my father's left hand at Sheriffmuir. "Let it remind you, lad. No sheep ever saved his throat by bleating. But harken to this, Colin. It's dead important. You'll still run, lad, if it comes to that. I'll not have you killed in your first battle. Your mother'd not forgive me, nor could I forgive myself. And you'll be no bloody berserk—not at your age, not ever. You're lucky. You've killed no one"—to which I nodded assent—"and 'tis the best time to stop. I've killed people, but I'm not a killing man. Colin, no decent man cherishes memories of murder. He can only try to live in such a way as to be forgiven."

The next day we would march away to what was to be the first battle, and Colin Randall MacDonald was filled with the foolish notion that he might henceforth protect himself, come what may. I was a child then, and would remain so for another few hours. Meanwhile we three enjoyed that last evening camping outside Edinburgh, devouring the last good hot meal we would have for some time. I have often thought, when hunger crawled inside me like a centipede, that all human suffering might be cured by a generous portion of haggis. We had haggis that night, heated over the open fire, and a joint of meat Angus Og had found: good red meat turned at the point of my dirk, its juice dripping into the fire, sending up spurts of flame until the meat crinkled up and turned brown.

"I can't abide that smell much longer without taking action," said Angus Og, and Father and I agreed. So we ate heartily and washed it down with good Edinburgh ale and were merry. With the evening growing cold—what my mother would call a young friendly cold, teeth but no real bite—we curled up around the banked fire and slept.

# 6

*Toe River Trail*

SEPTEMBER 27, 1780

Despite snow already in the Blue Ridge, we have traveled sixty-five miles in three days. Luckily my feet have held up all these years, and far I walked thus as a boy, though we had no snow in those dowie days of harvest on the road to Prestonpans.

I recall on September 19 our patrols brought in a few of Cope's student volunteers. It was clear now that Cope truly was on his way. At the end of our three days of drill and hearty fare, the Grants from Glenmoriston arrived to join Charlie's army. It seemed a good omen.

When the prince rode out to Duddingston he held forth a naked sword. Standing before us, he cried out in that high-pitched, lisping way of his, "Gentlemen, I have flung away the scabbard. With God's assistance, I don't doubt of making you a free and happy people. Mr. Cope shall not escape us as he did in the Highlands." Amid a great shout, the air became a blizzard of blue bonnets. The scene might have given old Cope pause had he witnessed it.

At three of the clock the following morning, we moved

out in columns of three. The prince rode ahead, clad as an ordinary soldier, in coarse plaid and blue bonnet. Lord George was with him, then Lochiel and his Camerons. We joined the main road at Magdalen Bridge, passing through the market gate at Fisherrow and over the River Esk. The first sunlight sparkled in the street, and the people waved kerchiefs and flags. Our colors were broken out and we tried to keep in step with the pipers. One MacDonald had put a broom up on a pole to show how we'd sweep the English away. The prince had reined in his horse while the column trudged by, and when the banners and the standards passed he took off his bonnet, watching the flags moving ahead in the sunlight. It seemed to me there could be worse fates than to die fighting with those flags waving overhead.

Thirty years had passed since Scotland had fielded a Jacobite army. Very few of us had drawn a blade in anger, and I wondered aloud to my father how we would do.

"Don't fuss, laddie," he told me. "We'll do our duty." I wondered why he was so sure. "Och, love of the prince's cause will carry us through." Rumor had it that the prince meant to lead the first charge. "He believes he has a monopoly on God," my father said.

"And does he?"

"Just thinking so may help," Father said. "But I've come to suspect God is often fickle in these matters. He may give us a hand now and again, but once the bayonets come on, be ready to run or fight with all your worth, lad."

I told myself I meant to fight that day. If Father stood firm and Angus Og, too, then so must I.

With a shuffle and clink, we rolled along between stubbled Lowland fields down the Musselburgh road, then off on the Old Post Road. We were passing behind the gardens of Pinkie House, where in bygone days there had been a battle, when Lord George came posting back to lead us into the fields south of Wallyford. High ground lay ahead, and we made for the heights at a trot. I saw the prince riding by, shouting "Gres-ort, Gres-ort, make haste!" And where the slope flattened out toward Falside, we came to a panting halt.

Less than a mile away, where the plain resumed, drawn up rank after rank, was half a mile of living men in battle order, their flanks protected to the west by a long stone wall and on the other side by a ditch. Behind them shimmered the sea, above which hung the darker blaze of the sky. I heard the mutter of drums and far off a faint shout of defiance, like a flock of sea gulls calling. We yelled back, and some men even pounded on their targets.

Those who would fight in the old manner of Highlanders should always first seize the high ground, for the slope adds momentum to the charge and, as I would understand later, it absorbs the impact of artillery. Thanks to Lord George we now held such ground. We simple soldiers were ready to fling ourselves down helter-skelter upon the foe, and I believe the prince was eager, too, but Lord George sent a Colonel Kerr forward on a small white pony. He never flinched when the enemy fired upon him but moved thoughtfully before their lines, returning to report that the ground before us was a marshy meadow and virtually impassable.

The only excitement occurred when O'Sullivan, who was full of peculiar notions, sent fifty Camerons to occupy a church down below. Cope's artillery began using them for target practice until Lochiel appealed to Lord George, who called them back. We could spare no men from the assault before the night came on.

If Lord George countermanded the squandering of fifty men on a churchyard, you can imagine his reaction when he found out O'Sullivan and the prince had dispatched ten times that number to guard the Edinburgh road. Without so much as a by-your-leave, they had put five hundred of the best blades, Lord George's own Atholl men among them, entirely out of the fight.

What happened next shocked me at the time. It disturbs me still, the prince and Lord George face to face and Lord George almost snarling, pounding one clenched fist on the other, throwing his pistols on the ground and swearing before God he'd not draw sword again until his Atholl brigade was returned.

Lord George's fit was bad enough in any company, but the way the prince stood there and meekly submitted to a man who clearly despised meekness seemed far worse. If you ask me, this was when their bad blood began, with Lord George assuming a free hand without so much as paying lip service to the prince's generalship, and the prince beginning to sulk and to lend an ear to O'Sullivan's resentment.

In any event, by the time the Atholl brigade had formed up with the rest of us, the sun was low and no time remained to engage the enemy. Twelve hours of daylight was all one could expect toward the end of September, so we filed off into the stubble field from which the peas had already been harvested. Night fell, bringing with it the first frost, and the two armies settled down with the Tranent bog between them.

We silently wrapped ourselves in our plaids with a handful of pea straw for a pillow. No fires were lit that night—not even in the prince's bivouac—but down below great campfires flowered in the dark like red blossoms. To inspire his men, I suppose, or to warn us he was on guard, Cope fired off an occasional mortar while the night took on a cold edge. In Tranent village a dog barked in alarm, sparking off a spatter of shots. Cold mist rolled in from the sea and sleep came hard, even to a boy unaccustomed to wakefulness. I kept remembering the prince's humiliation and thinking that no one talks to royalty that way. No one.

I had barely drifted into shallow sleep when I was annoyed by a hand on my shoulder and Angus Og's insistent but always genial voice. "Colin! Wake up!"

Lord George and the prince had achieved a late-night reconciliation, thanks to one Robert Anderson, the son of a local laird, who had spent his boyhood snipe hunting in the Tranent marsh. He said there was a dry path over which he could lead the army in the dark. Lord George favored this idea and had tactfully proposed it to the prince, who was delighted.

One problem remained, and one last argument. I'm sorry to say it was MacDonalds this time, claiming their privilege of holding down the right flank. This caused grumbling all around and much shuffling back and forth before we got going again, feeling our way like sleepwalkers in the dark before dawn.

While leaping a ditch, the prince fell to his knees in the mud. He bounded up quickly with a grin, but this worried the superstitious, and when a sow scuttled across our path—another bad omen—the front rankers slew her with their dirks. I'm not one to credit these old notions, but I did feel alarm when a government dragoon shouted, "Who goes there?" In the misty dark he must have accepted silence as a proper response, for no alarm was spread.

The crackle and rustle of the freshly cut stubble finally gave us away, that or the coming dawn, for our attack was not a surprise as some said later, and the Sassenach had a chance to form up and shift their line while our officers were calling on us to close up. Hamilton's Dragoons rode up on the left. Infantry held the middle of their line, Lee's regiment and that of Lascelles among others, with artillery rumbling on the right. I could see bayonets glinting in the dawn light, and in the face of this English power we should, by right, have been driven from the field.

Our pipers, Father and Angus Og among them, sounded the rant, and Alexander MacDonald stepped out ahead, making a little steadying gesture with the flat of his hand. I'm not sure a command was ever given, any more than to a flood that bursts through a dam. Lochiel's Camerons were simply off with a rush into the melting mist, heading for the artillery. Then all the rest had to follow.

For a moment the government line was a solid crescent of red pricked out with flashing points of steel. A volley cracked out, then billowing smoke studded the pricks of light. The clans came on howling, heads low behind targets, claymores brandished. Here and there a flag danced wildly and the enemy began giving ground, backing off slowly at first, and then the jostling began and the panic grew. I'm not sure the English even tried to reload. Our men gave them no time, throwing aside their plaids and plunging into the government line with the cry of howling wolves.

We MacDonalds of Glencoe were in the second line and holding fast until Angus Og dropped his musket and leapt ahead, shouting a battle cry that had not been heard since Sheriffmuir. Not to be outdone, a good many others plunged after him.

The fact is, I'd been ordered to remain back with the humblies. Even so, I recall how my mouth went dry and my hands began to sweat when we moved forward, too, walking at first, then trotting, my heart beginning to pound like the devil's drum. My legs seemed to have gone all stiff in the thighs. I had trouble making them work at first, but excitement and concern for my father and Angus kept me going. No one tried to stop us, and I realized the first charge must have entirely swept the field. Veiled in coppery shreds of mist, the hills and housetops seemed to be catching fire as the whole long line of us pounded forward with our dirks and scythes, not so much into our first battle, for that was done—all save the slow dying—but into victory.

Only gradually did I become aware that the moor smelled of gunpowder, sweat, and something else—blood—and all about me there was moaning. We Highlanders had few casualties at Prestonpans—only a handful of officers had fallen—and call it Fate if you wish, but I stumbled over one of them who was kin to me. It was the only time we met in this life, for he was sorely wounded. Captain James MacGregor lay before me, holding himself together. His face was as stiff and hard as an image stamped on a silver coin. Needing someone to listen, he grasped my hand and told how he was one of Rob Roy's several sons and hence my mother's cousin. He recognized my father's name and swore they had once been together on a raid into Menzies and Campbell land. Taking note of my scant equipment, he added, "Young Colin, there's no borrowing a sword in wartime, but I'll trust ye to carry this one of mine till I'm back on my feet." He nudged his broadsword toward me. A fine west Highland beaknose it was. "I'll keep it safe until you're mended," I echoed, though I think we both knew better.

"Draw it only with honor, laddie. Only with honor." And that was the last he said to me.

I lingered awhile, but no more passed between us. Captain MacGregor was through with this world and I could but wish him well on his journey to the next, while wondering if it was worthwhile to give one's life for Charlie. Was winning a battle ever worth that price? No dead man will ever tell you yea or nay, but I must think so, or I would not be here. Regardless, I will tell you this: Even as clear a victory as we had just won brings less joy than the old poetry tells. I'd suffered no hurt, held a fine sword in my hands; and yet I was crying, having learned one thing: Next to a battle lost, the saddest thing is a battle won.

All those wounds and the pain never find their way into the poems and songs. When a Highlander fights with his broadsword, it's no tidy punching of bullet holes but a wild hacking and slicing by men in their battle fury, a mad butcher's business. Some of our men had the notion that the government horses were trained to fight like soldiers, so they went for them with dirks. You hardly know about agony until you've heard horses screaming by the dozens.

I'll give the prince credit: He tried to stop it, not just because we needed horses but from an old-fashioned notion of chivalry, I believe. When he came up from the reserves he looked honestly distressed at the slaughter of the wounded and the animals, and he began shouting, "Take prisoners! Spare them! They are my father's subjects, too!"

Not that he was all compassion, for presently I saw him eating heartily in the midst of that bloody field and laughing aloud at how his Highland men had lost their plaids. I suppose half-naked men seeking out their clothing after a battle has its humorous side—that and our prisoners wandering about with their red coats turned inside out. I was told there were a good seven hundred such, with half as many wounded, for whom the duke of Perth had sent for doctors.

I might have enjoyed our victory more if I had known what had become of my father and Angus Og. I dreaded the possibility that they were among the dead carpeting the ground, like so many dummies flung down by God from a vast height. They seemed so very dead, like the mice left chewed and stiff on the doorstep by our family cat. I suppose I felt superior to the English that day, but mostly I felt superior to the dead, and but for Angus and my father I would have quit the field.

It was not long before I found them, with not a mark on either that would not wash off. The two of them were grinning so widely they seemed to be lit from inside. I must have been beaming, too, with relief.

"Here's a stout heart," my father said, clapping an arm around my shoulder, "with a blade all your own, I see. And this Angus, he's a holy terror when the pipes begin to play." Angus's sword was red and it slid sandily back into its scabbard. "He's killed more Sassenachs than the Black Death."

The three of us helped move the wounded that afternoon to Bankton House, and if Angus Og had hacked them with a fury that morning, there were tears in his eyes for the helpless foe that afternoon. There was no other hospital, and for all our efforts, by no means all of the government wounded got to the surgeons that day or the next.

"It's an old, old way," Father said, speaking of the greedy quest for booty that engaged so many who might have helped the wounded or buried the dead. He made a joke about the Highlander who seized a gold watch, then threw it away when the spring ran down, saying, "I'm glad to be rid of the creature, for she lived no time at all after I caught her." When I didn't laugh, Father said, "Dinna fash yourself, laddie. You'll know what to expect next time."

"I hate so many terrified eyes all staring at me."

"Yon Sassenachs?"

I nodded. "It makes me wonder if there's something wrong with me."

Then Father lowered his own eyes and said softly, "So you've lost your youth and come to manhood all in a morning, Colin. That's hurtful, that is, but you'll learn a soldier must have a heart of stone, or no heart at all." Nearby, a horse teetered on three legs, eating stubble. "But now the battle's done, and thank God a great victory's been won."

He was right, of course. The prince was in command of Scotland save for a few small government forts and the castles of Stirling, Dumbarton, and Edinburgh. Prestonpans would find its way between heavy leather covers, but I would come to realize it was only the victory of one weak little army over another.

"Poor Johnnie Cope will never live it down," Father said with a smile, and I guess he never did. In large measure thanks to my father's rhymes, Cope was remembered as the commander who carried the panicked word of his own defeat into England. Some of our men wished to hound him there, but we were but a few thousand warriors with winter at hand, and no sign of a French fleet to help us in an alien land. Perhaps we were invincible. Charlie seemed to think so, and he would have chased Cope to Coldstream and on to Berwick, but at the first muster it became clear we'd lost more men to booty and loot than to the enemy. All the remainder of us could do was line up and trudge back to Edinburgh. This sat well enough with most of us, who had little stomach for pursuing an English crown into a distant and alien land.

Camerons led the way. Their pipers played the usual, "When the King Enjoys His Own Again," and others down the line joined in. Captured standards and our prisoners brought up the rear. We paraded in triumph through the city streets, and I began to forget about the wounded and delighted in having a sword. This was heady excitement, though not for a boy, unless he wants to grow up fast and forget about being a boy.

"Do you think we'll be going home?" I asked my father.

"Not yet awhile, I'll wager," he replied.

"Not even for the winter?"

"Nay, lad. Destiny means to build the future of our island upon this war." He said this solemnly, reminding me of my mother for an instant, then smiling. "And we'll be needing a new tune to goad them with. Something about how we met Johnnie Cope in the morning. Aye, something like that." Before the prince's year was done, every piper in our army was playing that tune. I hum it still sometimes. As for Johnnie Cope himself, we never saw hide or hair of him again.

# 7

We had marched back to Edinburgh in triumph, but then the word came down to stifle our enthusiasm, since we had after all, defeated the king's subjects and they were not to be humiliated. In truth we had little chance or reason to gloat, having been posted out to Duddingston again, where recruits kept pouring in and conditions were going from bad to worse. The prince had requisitioned more tents, but they scarcely went around, and I can still recall how the bugs crawled over my face in the night. It was small consolation that young women flocked there by day to cheer on our drilling, and we all gave three hearty cheers when the camp was abandoned and we were moved back to the city.

There the castle was still holding out against us. I believe the government hoped to keep Charlie busy besieging the place, and after an exchange of fire, which set a few houses ablaze in the city, another cease-fire was arranged.

In the high councils, we were told, the prince was urging a rapid march south, which Lord George opposed so long as our numbers were small. O'Sullivan, it was said, whispered in Charlie's ear that Lord George was a Hanoverian at heart. This was never so, if you ask me. Our big mistake was in counting on France. Since long before the days when

Mary, Queen of Scots, had been wed to the dauphin of France, there had existed the Auld Alliance, as we called it, and there was confident talk of the French army flocking to our victorious colors. A few French ships did cross the Channel, and the marquis d'Eguilles arrived at Stonehaven to advise the prince that the duc de Richelieu was on his way with twelve thousand men, which eased our doubts about marching south.

So while we waited, many slunk off out of homesickness or to get in the harvest. Had Father or Angus chosen to do so, I might have, too, and I wonder sometimes, would it have made a difference? Many stayed on for fear of their chiefs. Because victory is always a great magnet, many more came in to swell our Jacobite army. All the world loves a winner, and the prince was not the sort to accuse a man for a sudden change of heart. Lord Ogilvie brought six hundred men, and when Gordon of Glenbucket arrived from Aberdeenshire, four hundred swords followed him. Mackinnon of Skye fetched one hundred and twenty, and on the ninth day of October Lord Pitsligo arrived with one hundred and thirty-two horse and nearly double that in foot soldiers. We were becoming an army to be reckoned with, but one with a belly, too. The farms around Edinburgh were hard put to sustain us. French ships did bring some food, but never the troops they had promised.

There was a steady coming and going of visitors, some of whom came to join the army and follow it come what may. Others stayed only briefly. Mary, Peggy, and Mother arrived as a complete surprise. I remember kissing all three of them in the old way, joyfully on both cheeks. October was already in its waning days. "Bide awhile," my father said, but the herd and the harvest needed them, and five days was all they could afford. Man of the world that I'd become, I showed Peggy Edinburgh.

"And soon you'll be on your way to London," she said.

"I hope not," I told her.

"So I've heard," she replied with a questioning smile, as though she did not credit half of what the world told her.

"Not till the French come," I said, "and your brother says they won't."

"Och, Colin, you look so angry."

"Not with you," I insisted.

"See how your hands are fists. Colin, open them, give them here." She seized my hands. "I wish you were one of the village babies, so I could make you stay safe at home. I could look after you." Two spots of color burned in her cheeks.

"I'm a soldier now, Peg. I'm where I have to be." I blush now, remembering such pomposity, but at the time it was more than serious. Though Peg brushed it off with, "Will you harken to that, now," her voice sounded as though she were about to cry.

The three of them were away back to Glencoe on the twenty-fifth. The following day we moved to a camp west of Inveresk church. Everyone asked why. To make room for the French troops? Hardly anyone believed that. Supposedly the prince wanted to march on Newcastle and attack the government army there under General Wade, but Lord George was holding out for Carlisle, where a band of English Jacobites supposedly awaited our coming. In any event, winter was drawing nigh. The flood of recruits was drying up, and men would soon be wandering off faster than they came in, while the English armies would keep on returning from Flanders to bar our way. Even I realized that if we were to march south, it had to be soon, and on the last day of October 1745, that march began. There were thirteen regiments of us now, followed by sixteen cannon and a few carriages, including those of Lady Kilmarnock and Lord Ogilvie's young and beautiful wife. Less highborn women walked, some helping with the baggage train and our cattle. Lord Elcho's horse guards led the way as flags were unfurled from their casings. At least six thousand strong, we looked more like an army than we ever had before, or would again.

Two columns set out, the prince taking the Jedburgh road while the rest of us marched by way of Peebles and Moffat to confuse the English spies who were watching. As I had been a herdsman at home, I helped to drive the black cattle. A cold rain had begun to fall. I knew that in the mountains back home it must be falling as snow.

The land of Scotland narrows sharply where the River Esk empties into the Solway Firth. Frontiers are strange to me. There is seldom a sudden change in the nature of the land, no difference between one bank of a river and the other, save in men's minds; yet one side was Scotland, a place a Highlander like myself would unhesitatingly defend, the other England and therefore alien, where Scots seldom prospered and often died.

My father's ballads sing of Flodden Field, where so many of our ancestors perished, and Otterburn, which saw the great James Douglas fall even as he won the day. Not far away at Philiphaugh, Montrose, who had never lost a Highland fight regardless of the odds, saw his army cut to pieces and his hopes dashed forever. These were only a few, but my father had not one song to sing of Scottish victory south of the Esk. Still, we were about to cross it yet again.

The autumn wind punished us with frosty fingers as we headed down the bank. The River Esk is neither deep nor wide, but the water was so cold it burned, until the hurt went deep down and deadened feeling. Here and there were ominous ripples and furrows warning of the rapid current. One of the cannons chose to topple down the bank, snapping a gunner's leg. This was seen as a dark omen. Once safely over, many of the men drew their swords, holding them up toward Scotland in salute. As Lochiel did so to encourage his clan, he cut his hand, another gloomy portent to all who observed or heard of it.

Otherwise the crossing went well enough and we marched on at a good pace, what with a goodly portion of our baggage left behind at Lockerbie. They say it took our column three hours to pass at any one point, and the English farmers looked on silently. Towns were even slower going, for King James's proclamation had to be read aloud. Those who listened seemed more puzzled than delighted.

On the ninth day of November the two columns came together north of Carlisle. This had been the intention all along, but instead of picking up Lowland recruits along the way, it was a sorry thing to see how the ranks had thinned with desertions. Yet the prince seemed in high spirits, rising with the rest of us before dawn, encouraging the clans by again marching first with one, then with another, urging us on in that heavy, hissing Italian accent, which was confusing and charming at the same time. I do believe he had English, French, Italian, and Gaelic all mixed up, but still with his hands and expressions he had a way of drawing people to his side. Even though I could not understand him exactly, I fancied he saw us sharing a great and sacred mission. Angus Og maintained that the prince was a selfish manipulator, using us as he would any useful tool, But even looking back this judgment seems needlessly harsh to me.

I believe the prince honestly expected English Jacobites to flock to us. I'm not sure why. The land looked prosperous, and if King George was being hard on his subjects it did not show.

Even when they did not join us we never abused these

people. A few sheep may have been eaten without proper payment at Brampton, where the prince set up camp hoping to draw General Wade out of Newcastle, but nothing more than that. Yet I believe they thought we Highlanders had the stomachs of wolves and would eat their babes raw. In truth the daughter of a bishop got down on her knees to plead for her infant's life, till a Captain MacDonald swept off his cockade and said, "Let the babe be christened with this cockade in her cap. It will be a protection now and after if any of our stragglers come this way."

Martinmas Saturday found us just north of Carlisle. As the market day crowd came and went neither side chose to open fire. Next morning, however, the guns of the castle blazed away into the heavy fog. I suppose the garrison hoped to frighten us off until General Wade came to relieve them. Now, a great deal was going on behind the scenes that I did not know about at the time. General Wade had hundreds of sick men on his hands, and when snow began to fall he gave up on rescuing Carlisle and sent a messenger to tell the garrison so. Meanwhile, Lord George was working on another tantrum because he didn't like so many of our people twiddling their thumbs in Brampton. He wanted every man jack of us digging entrenchments for the siege of Carlisle, and I've mentioned how Highlanders take to the shovel. A few more wandered off to avoid the indignity, till the duke of Perth shed his coat, grabbed a shovel, and shamed some of us into digging. About this time, what with Lord George's grumblings, the prince gave up on Brampton and pitched in with the rest of us. He seemed to enjoy himself.

The fourteenth brought heavy snow, and with the air smelling of more snow to come, the city garrison offered to surrender. They were naught but a band of freezing old men yearning for their hearths, some said. Yet the prince must have felt we were an invincible army as he rode into

59

town with all the pipers playing. I would have agreed with him. No matter that some fifteen hundred men had wandered off, that winter was upon us, that Carlisle Castle was crumbling and its garrison a handful of old militia, that there was no sign of the French, or that three government armies were waiting in our path. Prince Charlie was ready to take on London, and so was I, and this time we had our way, marching south on the twenty-first in two divisions again, Lord George commanding one and the prince the other. The only ominous sight was having to leave a hundred of our men behind to guard the city walls. Carlisle was reckoned to be full of Jacobites, yet hardly a one volunteered to help guard the castle, much less march with the rest of us to glory.

The prince had us up at dawn each day. It was said he slept little and was stumbling with fatigue, but few armies have moved at such a pace. A few more deserted as we neared Preston, for Scots are great ones for seeing history repeating itself, and here it was that the rising of 1715 had been snuffed out. Not this time. Bells rang to welcome us, but only a handful of recruits turned out, and few in the watching crowd cheered or even smiled as Lord George marched us steadily through town and across the icy Ribble to set up camp at Wigan, which was haunted by no Scottish ghosts.

By now, Father was guessing we would head straight on to Manchester, a Jacobite city if there was one in England, while Liverpool, which lay along the other possible route, was said to have locked its gates against us.

Penrith and Lancaster, some of the smaller towns, lit bonfires and rang their church bells to honor us, but enlistments were few. The roads were becoming muddy and soft as a plowed furrow, obliging us to take to the fields. A good many bridges had been dismantled in our honor and the fords were swollen with water so cold it felt like iron fingers kneading my bones. Each river crossed was one more river between me and home. I didn't talk about that, but most of us thought about it and a good many continued to vanish. Most of the tents had been left behind, so it was sleep out or spend half the night hoping the officers could settle us on some fearful villager who no more wanted Highlanders on his hands than we wanted to be there.

"It's not so different than Scotland here—the Lowlands, anyway," I told my father.

"And should it be, lad?" he answered back. When I did not reply, he added, "You wait till you see London. Then you tell me how 'tis all the same."

I was in no hurry, not caring to see what I knew would be diminished by grander sights. In the end I did see London, in a way I would not have imagined even in my darkest nightmares.

We had gotten the idea—I guess it went back to Prince Charlie—that the old Catholic families of North Wales, Lancashire, and Cheshire would welcome us with open arms, but few of their sons turned out, and Angus began calling the prince a fool who knew not his friends.

We lacked spies to match the English, but we had scurriers on horseback who saw enough. General Wade, who knew the Highlands and had our respect, was east of the Pennine Mountains. Another army of militia was said to be gathering on Finchley common to defend London, and then there was Cumberland. Cumberland, the king's son, back from the continental wars and gathering his army at Litchfield. All these armies groping for us, and at the time I feared none of them so long as we could meet them one by one like Johnnie Cope.

"They say this Cumberland is a fighter," Angus Og said, and we talked of a meeting between him and Charlie alone, the two princes hand to hand in single combat. It seemed fitting, somehow, the two of them of equal rank and age with about the same stake in the outcome, though even Angus agreed that Charlie would win such a match, for the duke of Cumberland was said to be soft and fat, and our Charlie, for all his flaws, was an athlete.

Our prince wore a kilt with a blue sash and his blue velvet bonnet to ride into Manchester. Bells and bonfires awaited us and a cheering crowd escorted him to his lodgings, but if Charlie inspired Highland hearts he never seemed to win over minds south of the border. Instead of a whole new army of gentlemen joining us there, about two hundred rough unemployed fellows turned out, and these unarmed vagabonds became the Manchester regiment. Compared to that ill-begotten lot, we looked like a king's bodyguard.

I had spoken to the prince once before, as you know, when he marched with the MacDonalds. We would stand face to face again before the issue was decided, and I would know him as a traveling companion before Charlie's Year had run its course, but I deem what was said at Manchester, and what was left unsaid there, the most important.

The exchange took place in the street. I suppose you might say he was sampling our resolve, and it began with him addressing me in the crowd of gawking Highlanders who stood there. "Here, boy. We've met before, have we not?"

"Aye, Your Highness, on the road to Blair."

"One of my veterans, then, and I esteem your opinion all the more. Tell me, how would you have me lead you into London? On horse, or on foot? In court dress or kilt?" I told him on horse, so as to be seen, and in court dress, which would appear less foreign, to which he replied, "I like talking to you Highlanders. You answer direct and to the point. And what of yourself, how would you march in?"

"As you see me, for I have no other," I told him, "but I would be scrubbed if given a choice."

This made him laugh, and he replied, "And so you shall." He scribbled out a note, giving me passage into his own headquarters. "See that you shine like a fresh-struck farthing before we pass over London Bridge," he told me, and then he was on down the street, stiffening the backbone of others, for he knew how to use his Highlanders and got the best out of each one of us.

A couple of days' rest in Manchester saw us marching again, with as many more veterans deserting as we made up from the ragtag of the Manchester regiment. I didn't know then how reluctant the chiefs were in pressing on, with the enemy closing around us. At Macclesfield the rumor got about that Cumberland was approaching, with an army twice our size. It must have been true, for Lord George took a large company apart, leading a diversion as though he meant to storm through Wales. Cumberland, they say, was taken in by this feint: He moved to block it and let the rest of us tramp to Derby on the London road.

London. I could fairly smell it, and only the tattiest sort of militia trembling in our way at Finchley. Our oat bags had all been filled at Manchester, and if rich men ate at their will, and poor men when they could, we were not starving, nor daunted by the weather, and when a few flakes of snow fell I caught one on my tongue, where it burned.

Derby lay just ahead. Some of the bridges on the way were broken down, and the townspeople had raised funds for the government cause. But when Lord Elcho and his life guards led the way to the market square, the Derbyshire Blues, who had pledged themselves to hold us off, melted away and the folk there looked on in panic as our rough, dirty, threadbare, and sometimes shoeless rabble took charge. Let it be written here, as it has been before, that we did them no injustice.

Night had fallen before the prince arrived in town. Then the colors were broken out, the white banners crossed in red, and my father together with the others piped him down Full Street to his lodging at Exeter House. Spirits were high. Cumberland had been outwitted, and if the militia at Finchley did not fly along with the Derbyshire Blues, they would be quick work for our broadswords. The cutler shops in Derby never did a better business as we cleaned and sharpened our already clean and sharpened blades. I am not ashamed to admit that I was among them, and Father only nodded when he saw me there, for he knew, as I did, that our final victory could change the world, must change the course of history, or we would have no victory.

Perhaps it was admiring that bright blade or sensing that London was upon us that caused me to act upon the pass the prince had presented me, and I boldly approached Exeter House. Daunted at the last by the elegant throng that filled the inn's front room, I went around to the kitchen entrance, where the pass worked like the proverbial charm. I soon found myself ensconced and alone, up to my neck in suds in what could only be the inn's pantry, with no more than an occasional waiter to intrude upon my self-indulgence.

I might scarcely recall that bath, the only one I ever had on English soil, had not a small serving panel stood open a crack on the room beyond, which I deemed to be a large oak-paneled drawing room, which was full to the brim with those men who had led us here, including Prince Charles. They all seemed to talk at once, and I made no sense of it at first. Then it was Charlie's distinctive voice insisting that a French fleet proposed to land troops in December.

"What proof? What proof have you?" Lord George was asking, but clearly he was not interested in a reply but was building up to the point he meant to press. "No proof whatsoever, yet I can tell you that our four thousand men are now opposed by some thirty thousand English. Your Highness, surely it is time to think of what must be done."

"What must be done? March on, of course," the prince told him. The room held its breath. Outside I heard Scottish voices shouting from the street. "Listen, gentlemen. They call for London."

"Not one, if he knew the facts," Lord George said coldly. "Show me that one man. Show me one man in this room foolhardy enough to cry, 'On to London,' and I will march at your side."

Silence. I can still recall that troubled, terrible silence, and then the prince spoke again, high-pitched and tremulous. Then a sudden picture came into my head. Imagine this: a boy of fourteen naked as a needle but for a small towel, suddenly plunging into that stately room lit only by the coppery light of the great fireplace, shouting, "On to London." All those famous men struck dumb, as when you toss a rock into a pond full of croaking frogs.

I had that chance to change history but did not. I only sank deeper into the hot water of my tub and felt miserable. I was as clean as I had ever been in my life, but suddenly I felt dirty.

In such moments it is the small details that stick in the mind, and while Lord George was guaranteeing a safe return to Scotland I was staring into a steamy mirror. I had not seen my face in a long time, and so I considered myself and my lips formed words. "Och, Colin, 'tis no business of yours," I cautioned myself while still imagining a naked, steaming lad rushing in to change the tide while the prince was being cornered and broken. He did fight back, shrill and lisping. "In future I shall be accountable only to God!" Then a heavy door slammed shut and the prince was giving

65

orders in the kitchen. "Surely you can find one bottle of brandy. I really must have some brandy." I was ready to sink under the water entirely, but he did not come in. No one did, so I dried myself off and that was that.

Was it all for the best? Perhaps. Who knows? I might never have found my way home again, never seen my Peggy, and yet I shall always wonder. Such thoughts went around and around in my head as I wandered back to the stable where they had billeted the MacDonalds of Glencoe. I must have looked tired, for my father said to me, "Don't let the world get you down, Colin."

"You needn't worry about me," I replied, but I said no more to him nor to Angus Og, who only spoke ill of the prince. It was a dank night, and in the straw we had no fire. Against the one window, fog pressed like a lonely ghost. A few men still spoke excitedly of the victory to come and London, the younger ones kneading their hands together and nodding at what the older ones said. But I had had all the adventuring I needed for one night. I was played out and said naught of what I knew.

So many years ago and still I wonder. Did a fourteen-year-old lad have a chance to change the course of the Jacobite war? Not likely, yet it is a thing to ponder. And did Prince Charles have the right to take such a risk? A leader's risk is the risk of all. Who can say? I might have answered yes at the time, thinking only a miracle could pull us through against the odds and believing at the time, as I have said, that our Charlie was a bit of a miracle. Surely up until Derby he was the only trump card we held. Was it play him or throw away the game? Don't ask me, but you have to admit it makes a good story, how I had a chance to win the Jacobite war and did not take it, but settled for a tub full of suds instead.

# 8

*The McDowell Plantation*

SEPTEMBER 30, 1780

We have been joined here by Colonel Benjamin Cleveland and Major Joseph Winston and their men. Tomorrow, rumor has it, we press on to the South Mountain gap, though the weather has a dire look. Thank the Lord it is not so cold as that sixth of December in '45.

That "Black Friday" began the long retreat from Derby in the dark before dawn. So dark it was that few realized at first we had passed this way before. I guessed early on, and looking about I saw no sign of Prince Charlie, though they said O'Sullivan was mistaken for the prince and fired upon.

Any number of stories went the rounds. We were off to meet the French at last, or seeking a field to do battle with General Wade. If our leaders were out to bewilder us that day, they were doing just fine. Morale was low, and consternation spread with the dawn. Retreat, we were assured, was a necessary evil—the first of what proved a whole succession of necessary evils—and you can't tell me, even now, that the march on London was doomed. Doomed or no, it would have settled things, and better than going there in chains later on as so many of us did.

Midday had come before the prince galloped by, ignoring our shouts and questions. Throughout the retreat he rose late, then rode on quickly to the next campsite, leaving Lord George to urge on the rear guard. Wherever Charlie went he'd inspired admiration. Now he was being thought of with caution, as one who might destroy himself in an excess of rage and wrongheaded courage. I heard he'd said of this change of plan, "I'd rather be twenty feet underground than see this day."

Behind him rode his adjutant general, the fat and jouncing John William O'Sullivan with jowls red as a cock's comb. "Look ye," Angus Og called after him, "yon's a bloody terror. Grab onto your belly button, Your Lordship, before you burst with fear!"

Poor O'Sullivan got no respect and deserved no more than he got. I laughed, though it did little to lift the depths of my concern. I wasn't the only one. The adjutant never turned his head, yet he'd have his revenge on all of us by and by.

The pace seemed to quicken with each passing day. Orders came down that if we abandoned so much as a cannonball the prince would go back and retrieve it personally. Still, things were being left behind. To pursue is one thing, to flee another. It wasn't just the idea that straggling might lead to being slain in a ditch, but there is a furious momentum in flight, like children who turn their backs on the terrors of the night and begin to run. A few horses were stolen from roadside farms to hasten escape for fear of cutthroats, and pretty soon throats really were being cut for horse thieving. And so it went, with the rear guard beginning to complain of Charlie's late habits and strange air of detachment, as if he had given up the struggle, though some said he delayed so as to prompt an engagement with Cumberland.

Still Lord George hounded us along, finding such food and shelter as he might. Prices were high, for the farmers assumed with good reason that we were beaten, and they preferred to jeer and throw stones when they dared. So we plodded back through Ashbourne and Manchester, where no bells rang. Rain fell as we arrived at Shap village to hear that the prince and his advance party had eaten them out of house and home. Still, Lord George rounded up some cheese and stale bread, which we toasted on the tips of our claymores.

After Shap it turned cold. Ice on the rutted roads did not help, and the sky took on the color of soiled iron. A few flakes of snow pelted down with a kind of sigh. "Mind this weather," my father said. His voice was soft and husky; all the weariness had risen to the surface. "There's a bonnie storm coming. You can feel it in your nose. Aye, and hear the wind." There was a high singing sound up in the tumbling gray rollers.

By now all rumors save the pell-mell reality of retreat had been scotched, and the only good thing about that white road upon which we plodded was the growing certainty that it led to Scotland.

The days were cold and the nights colder still. I felt as though I was made of wood. All feeling gone, you might have peeled me like a potato, and it made little difference that Glencoe must by now be a howling funnel of snow. It was home.

We'd seen English dragoons behind us or riding our flanks before, but not until Penrith were we really overtaken. English horsemen against Lord George's tough, hardened, battle-tried veterans. It wasn't much of a contest. The dragoons opened fire in the dusk and our men fired back at the flashes of their guns, then went in with their broadswords, and those dragoons who weren't chopped into mincemeat took off at a gallop.

Carlisle came next, on December 19, and Charlie was strutting out front again. He'd had more promises from France, and Lord John Drummond was said to be raising men and money in Scotland. But we lost four hundred men and most of our cannon to Carlisle. Lord George was for blowing up the castle and having done with the place, but the prince couldn't bear to give back all of England. The Manchester regiment, not very anxious to continue into Scotland, and a few others volunteered to garrison the city.

December 20 saw us back at the River Esk. It was swollen with all the rain and snow of recent days and we feared that men would be swept away, but there was no choice. The pipers lined up on the bank and began to play as we started down.

"There's ice in the water," my father said, to which Angus replied, "Aye, there would be every filthy thing today," but we plunged in with a will, because Scotland began on the far shore; and many a Highlander, as he went into that water, paused, turned, and spat back upon England. With the water up to our chests, we crossed all clinging together, as many as twelve abreast, like so many phantoms moving in the white plumes of our own breath. Not a man of us was lost in that wild surge of frigid water, yet two of the brave lassies who'd accompanied us so far were carried off.

Once ashore in Scotland, fires were lit, blazing up at the water's edge and seeming to cast a layer of orange oil across the river. I was so cold I wanted to jump into the flames, but we danced instead to reels that the pipers played, for we were safe home. It was Charlie's twenty-fifth birthday as well, and he was with us again, speaking bold words of how it was no retreat at all but a strategic withdrawal to

70

join the French and fresh forces raised in the north. A grand celebration was had on the north bank of the Esk that day. To see us prancing there you'd have thought we'd won the war.

It was like that for the next few days, on to Annan by the sea and Lockerbie, where we'd lost the supply wagons. We were put on the alert to reclaim them but saw only the village idiot crouching behind a gravestone in the cemetery, an ill omen for someone. Then on to Dalveen, with a halt at Douglas Castle and a hunt for Prince Charles in the duke of Hamilton's deer park. From there it was an easy march to Glasgow, an English city at heart, which met us with silence and sour gaze. This was Christmas Day, but no mangers had been set aside for Charlie's army, and he ordered the town council to scratch up some 12,000 shirts, 6,000 coats, and 6,000 pairs of shoes and stockings for his barefoot, tattered army.

They could afford it, and for a week we settled in, with balls at Trongate for the officers and gentlemen, and Prince Charlie sporting his finest French clothing again. A review of the army was held on Glasgow Green. We were only four thousand strong at this time, and a good many were sick with the ague and other complaints, while some had lost their weapons along the way. All the same, it was good to see the colors flying.

We were still an army, and spirits were high as we marched from Glasgow, Highlands bound. The mood didn't last, because the news caught up to us that Carlisle, what Lord George referred to as "that old hen coop," had fallen to the duke of Cumberland's heavy guns, with many of the garrison killed and the surviving officers to be tried for treason. So much for Stuart pride.

Most of us expected to move east, back to Edinburgh, but we trod on north to Stirling, while Cumberland went south again to intercept that illusive French invasion. General Wade still hibernated at Newcastle, but Edinburgh had been reinforced by General Henry Hawley, who was better known as "Hangman" Hawley, for he erected a gallows wherever he set up camp, as a sign he took discipline seriously.

The third day of January of 1746 brought us to Bannockburn again, below the walls of Stirling. I remember my feet were like two sores, and we settled down beside the swollen burn that murmured all night like an old grandfather talking in his sleep.

The prince called for a siege, and the town with its crumbling walls gave up without a shot. Not so Stirling Castle, and though Lord George said it was a great waste of time, since our battery was lightweight at best and Highlanders were no more willing to degrade themselves by fetching sandbags than they had been to dig graves, a half-hearted siege got underway. It was something to do, and it might have been pursued with greater zeal had not the prince vanished from the scene. Influenza kept him in a feather bed for over a week at the mansion of Sir Hugh Patterson.

Meanwhile the army tried for what rest and comfort we could find, though there's precious little of either in a tent come January in Scotland. The siege lingered on, little more than a joke. We never did raise a battery above the castle ramparts, but on the bright side more recruits came in, the majority accompanying Lord John Drummond and Lord Strathallan from Perth, so that we topped off at nine thousand strong, a high point in Prince Charlie's Year, which still had a few months to run.

Another, more personal, high point came with what we in the Carolinas call the January thaw. My mother, Mary, Peggy, and a few other women from the Glen, Loch Linnhe, and elsewhere came with food and good cheer for

72

their warriors bold. I remember ducking excitedly in and out of their arms, though I clung to Peg as long as seemed decent—that is, until she pulled away, and she didn't pull that hard.

Of course they had to hear about the march into England, and it was hard to explain the march back without fighting, much less losing a battle. I liked to think that the prince had come to his senses and decided to settle on Scotland, let England and Ireland go their own way, but my mother said, "Will ye harken to that now."

"That lad's right," my father told her. "We're here to stay."

"I hate contradicting the lot of you . . ." my mother replied, and I heard Father mutter, "Aye, it would be interesting to see what it would be like if you enjoyed it."

"Your sad old James," my mother continued, "he'll no come here to reign with England still at odds. And what will Charlie do? In the end he'll go back to Rome and leave the lot of you holding the bag."

"Hear the woman," my father said, his eyes flashing around, expecting support.

"Aye, 'tis the way of it," my mother said with finality, and though I was with Father in this, I'd seen the prince's odd behavior of late and was no longer sure of him.

Father went on to say that the war was about over, a standoff with us hanging on to Scotland, as it always used to be. Not so, replied my mother, into one of her far-seeing moods. She said Fate would never take so many precautions simply to let the matter rest. Destiny, like a tree, was planted in this war and would grow thereon, its branches shaping the future for Scotland and England alike. Oh, Mother, you were so often right and we so rarely listened. But that very day there were rumors that Hangman Hawley was on the move and meant to challenge us. Such news and the certainty that the January thaw must surely end caused the ladies to pack their few possessions and head for that home I would not see for months.

Each time it was harder to say farewell. I stood there long with my hands on Peggy's shoulders, leaning my forehead against hers, and I fancy she was too proud to cry, too proud of me to suggest I might come home.

"We'll be fine, lassie," I assured her, the mature veteran talking through my lips. She just kept her eyelids down so her face looked closed, and I reckon those who smile and wave recover ne'er so fast as those who weep.

My sister Mary asked me again to look after Angus Og. "He's my dear foolish bright-eyed man, and I want him back by and by." I promised not to return without him.

Then they were off, walking strong, and I longed to run after Peg. They hesitated just once to wave, and we waved back, with Father calling out, "Och, away you all go." Just then it seemed as though my heart had slumped off center, and had I been alone and not in the midst of an army I would have wept.

Hangman Hawley gave us scant time for sentiment. He was marching north, and January 15 found us, with pipes blaring, drawn up eight thousand strong at Plean Muir. To Lord George's disgust, a thousand men were left behind to continue the siege of Stirling's castle. Meanwhile, Hawley had marched through Linlithgow and on to a camp near Falkirk. From high ground we could see the glow of the English campfires.

Another battle was that near. Portentously I strapped on my broadsword. "You're going to draw such a grand old MacGregor blade in anger," my father observed, but this was not building up to a prohibition, for he went on like a ghostly echo: "Only mind, if you do, never dishonor it."

# 9

*The Gilbert Town Road*

OCTOBER 4, 1780

Yesterday William Campbell was officially elected commander of the Over Mountain Men. What irony that I, a MacDonald, voted for him, a Campbell. He's a great tall man, well over six feet, and a native-born Virginian who would be startled to know what enmity his name would have stirred in me during the winter of '46 when battle loomed before us.

We had expected to make battle with General Wade, but he had sulked in Newcastle, or with Cumberland, prince against prince, but Cumberland turned to meet the French, who never came. And now it was Hangman Hawley sallying forth from Edinburgh into bad weather. With him were the Royal Regiment—Wolfe's, Price's, Monro, Barrell, Battereau—all regiments of foot, eight thousand strong and a match for us in every way.

On the sixteenth day of January we marched from Plean Muir as the pipers struck up the new tune to which my father had contributed so many verses, "Hey, Johnnie Cope." A wild cheer went up and down the column, which

I would hear again on the muddy fields of war.

When Hawley declined to close the last miles between us, Lord George told us that while the English army might increase with delay, ours could only shrink, so we marched on to cross the cresting River Carron at Dunipace Steps, arriving in the night at Falkirk Muir. There the hill rises steeply to a moorland plateau of heather and scrub.

"We'll fight there on the morrow," my father said. " 'Twill be no Prestonpans this time. And you, Colin, armed with sword and dirk, be mindful that makes you no veteran, not yet awhile. Do remember that. It's dead important."

"I'm no daft," I replied, insulted. Oh, I was young then and knew no better. "I'm no wee bairn, either." It was settled in compromise. I was not to be in the front rank, but there was no talk of running away. There had, after all, been that talk about not dishonoring a hallowed blade.

"Look ye, lad, and remember this. If they come at you with a bayonet, you must fend it off somehow, with a target if you have one, or with your dirk if not. Then strike your blow. Do you understand?" My father's eyes held me, straight, honest, and searching. The moonlight made his features look haggard and drawn. "And this is dead important."

"I know," I interrupted impatiently, "never dishonor your sword." I knew, even as I spoke, that my sarcasm had hurt my father.

He sounded very tired and patient when he spoke again. "Aye, that too. But more important, if you must join in, remember it's far more dangerous to lose than to win." He tried to laugh, but the laugh broke up into a heavy cough that rocked him back and forth. For the first time in my youthful arrogance, I sensed that my father was paying a price for the long campaign.

Needing our strength, we tried to sleep. It was cold. The

76

air made me gasp. Though stars flashed overhead like swords, I half expected snow by morning. Fires were built, the same red and winking eyes, whether they warmed friend or foe that winter night.

January 17 dawned fair enough, but the southwest wind was building. The blue sky quickly turned to cast iron, becoming dark and threatening. No more shadows played over the hill, for all was shadow. I could only hope our ladies were safe home in the Glen, for it must already be storming there.

"Success to the White Rose," my father said.

"Confusion to the White Horse," Angus and I replied, touching our tin drinking cups.

Presently the army was in motion. We MacDonalds took the lead up Falkirk Muir and through all that remained of the once-great forest of Torwood. The ground was soft and growing softer from the thin black drizzle that hung low upon the crests. Gaining the high ground, we marched off to the right, and I heard my father draw a sharp breath as though he'd run a thorn under his fingernail. "Look! Yon's the Sassenachs!" He stooped and rubbed some dirt onto the grip of his sword. I did the same. Before us a long row of dragoons were ascending the far slope, not men and horses yet but tiny dolls. In the scudding rain, the heads of these dolls seemed detached from their bodies and their shouts came indistinct as church chimes on the wind.

"Are you fearful, laddie?" he asked me, and I nodded, not trusting myself to speak. "I'm glad you can admit it. Heaven help a man who can't on a day like this." He kept opening and closing his mouth in a hard, trembling yawn.

Up and down the line our pipes sounded the rant as the dragoons came on while that Highland wind veered, throwing an icy rain into their faces. My fingers curled around the hilt of my sword and my chest felt too small for my pounding heart. I remember an odd sensation, too, as though my feet floated lightly off the ground. My father's bagpipe faded with a sad belch and squeak as he cast it down to draw his sword.

A few muskets crackled in the torrent. Others refused. Still, a good many dragoons went down no more than ten yards from our front. As many more turned back, some plunged through to have dirks thrust upward into their horses' bellies. A nightmare crowd danced and pranced in the smoke of that deadly carnival, until the horsemen broke off entirely and fled down the hill.

I felt relieved and cheated, too. Another battle seemed over, and again I had not struck a blow. Then I saw that the slope below where the riders had passed was red with stumbling, running men and a red advancing flag. Sharp flames spat from a boiling haze of smoke, and our front rank cried out and leaped forward to meet them, and I was not far behind.

British bayonets and Highland broadswords crashed together and everyone seemed to be attacking his neighbor. I felt myself borne away in what must have been a battle fury. There was no room for rules of combat or what I'd been taught about using a broadsword. There was just this nightmarish hacking at things seen through a twilight of bright slashing blades. I brought the edge down on something that gave way. Then the ground under my own feet seemed to slide. I must have been struck with the butt of a gun, and I was down with a lobsterback over me, aiming a musket straight in my face. He pulled the trigger with a fierce grunt, as though dealing a blow with all his strength, but the lock would not fire. He tried again as I scrambled back, then came on with his bayonet until Angus battered in with his sword, shouting, delivering great cudgeling blows, and the Englishman collapsed, heavy as a tree that is felled with an ax.

The rain baffled a good many English muskets at Falkirk. Were it not for the weather and Angus Og's good right arm, I would never be writing now. In any event, my fighting was done for the day, for before I regained my feet the lobsterbacks had taken to heel, following their dragoons, with our clansmen in hot pursuit.

Feeling shaky and sick at my stomach, I did not follow. All around me lay twisted figures. To this day I don't know what I had to do with putting them there, but every muscle in my body seemed to be trembling. The dead looked strangely unreal unless I recognized a face, and few Highlanders were among the fallen at Falkirk. Yet the world was a blasted place, and I had helped make it so.

My throat hurt and was dry—from shouting, I suppose—and I buried my head in my arms, wanting to shut out all around me. Then I heard my father's voice hailing me, and I raised my head to see him toiling back up the hill.

"Naught's so bad, Colin. 'Tis another victory." He was breathing hard. At the sight of him I began to cry, and he admonished me, "Here, lad, you don't want to shame yourself before the others. They're rubbed up, too." So I dried my eyes with the back of my hand, though I didn't feel a bit better inside.

Soon Angus strode back up the hill as well, and I thanked him for helping me. "No harm will ever come to you through me," he said. "But that's a nasty bash you've got there on your forehead." I touched the bump, which had begun to throb.

"You look to have taken quite a clout yourself, Angus," I told him, for his lower lip was bloated and red like a damp sausage over his stubbling beard. We looked at each other and suddenly laughed out loud. I felt the blood rush into my face and turned away in confusion, since for no reason I'd begun to cry again.

Angus put his arm around my shoulder, and for a bit the shock was lost in his nearness. "Don't tell about this," I asked him, and then I noticed he was crying, too. I tried not to look, but he didn't care. "Let it out, lad, until you're free of it. Battles are an awful business, and it's best to get them out of your system."

"Ye might well say," I replied, glancing about at the fallen there, those who moved painfully and those who did not move at all. For the first time I saw my broadsword was stained and sticky in the grooves. "I guess we are the lucky ones," I observed, and, like a fool, I forgot to touch wood.

" 'Tis an awful thought, but a true one," Angus Og said. "The more I hate the pain and waste of this foolish war, the more I feel a need to draw my sword. Never again be a soldier, Colin, not if you can help it."

I didn't give it much thought at the time, but of course we'd won the battle of Falkirk. It hadn't lasted for more than twenty minutes, first to last. Some complained that we MacDonalds on the right had jumped too far ahead in the pursuit, but it seemed to be a deep ravine that had held up the Camerons and Frasers, the others who manned the left flank. In any case, there was no consistent pursuit. The drenching rain and the oncoming dark were no help, and then there was the booty to be collected. Hawley had tried to burn his tents and supplies, but the rain quenched the flames before much was destroyed. Hawley stormed off toward Linlithgow and then Edinburgh, where he took it out on Hamilton's dragoons for starting the panicky flight. He hanged over thirty of them, which was his nature, and saw as many foot soldiers shot for the same reason. That way Hawley didn't have to either blame himself or give us any sort of credit.

80

After the battle, the prince and Lord George had their usual disagreement. Lord George wanted to keep after the English—which I'll have to admit would have been difficult in that rain—while the prince wanted to get back to his siege of Stirling. This time the prince had his way, and he led most of the army back to Bannockburn and saw to it that a few siege guns were moved up to Gowan Hill, still a good fifty feet below the castle.

Lord George held the rest of us at Falkirk, where he secured the English tents, stores, and ammunition wagons. The rain kept up next day and we had to bury the dead in a muddy pit. It was ugly work. They had been stripped in the night, and by morning their white bodies on the slope looked like a flock of resting sheep. I believe I recognized the face of the man who'd aimed his musket at me, and I'd have brought him back to life there and then if I'd had the power.

That evening we marched back to Stirling. The moon poked holes in the clouds, and the castle on its hill glistened with frost. For over a week I helped cart sandbags up to protect the prince's battery on Gowan Hill. There was actually a French artillery expert in charge, but when the time came to open fire, toward the end of January, the government garrison in the castle fired back and blew our battery away in half an hour.

Only then did the prince say that perhaps we ought to chase General Hawley after all. It was too late, of course—and it wasn't just that. Many of our men had gone off with their plunder, which was the traditional way. The mood in our army was bad, what with the cold weather and poor food. Then there was an accident. Aeneas, young Glengarry's brother, was shot dead by one of the MacDonalds of Keppoch who was cleaning his musket. No malice was intended, and the dying man spoke words of forgiveness, but to stop a feud the MacDonald was shot. Nevertheless, dark feelings remained in both clans, and more men deserted.

So when Charlie met with his officers and talked about marching back to Edinburgh on the way to uniting the three crowns of England, Scotland, and Ireland for his father, none would support him. They say he banged his head on the wall in despair, but it was finally agreed we would retire farther north for the winter.

By this time the duke of Cumberland had arrived in Edinburgh to take over command. He was said to be a fat, rough-mannered young man and no military genius, but he did have experience of war and was sure of himself. His band played "Will Ye Play Me Fair, Highland Laddie, Highland Laddie" as he took the road north, one prince hunting another. It almost seemed that Destiny designed that final encounter, but if so, it might have done so with a more impartial hand.

We mustered that first day of February 1746, Highlanders, a few Lowland clans, and our Irish allies. Banners were broken out and pipes sounded up and down the line. Excitement gathered at the thought that we were off to meet Cumberland, a last desperate battle to have it done with one way or the other. It's strange but true: A battle is a terrible and terrifying business, but the life of a soldier is so drab and uncomfortable otherwise that I believe spirits plummeted as soon as it became clear we were marching north again, away from a fight.

I don't know if I believe in omens, but for those that do, there was a bad one that morning. I didn't see it, but I heard the rumble as the church of St. Ninians, which we'd been using to store powder, went up with a flash. Lord George declared it was an accident, and the prince kept silent. He didn't show his face to us that day or on any of the days that followed, while we plodded through Perth-shire to Crieff and Castle Menzies, and then through rain and snow to Blair Atholl. Instead of heading west, we kept on north as far as Inverness on the Moray Firth, where it would be easier for the French to reinforce us. I never caught a glimpse of the prince until we massed for battle one last time, and I never saw the French at all, though I must admit they have come to our aid here in the colonies, thirty years too late to help our bonnie Charlie.

# 10

*Near Denard's Ford on the Broad River*
OCTOBER 4, 1780

Ferguson and his Tory legion are not far ahead of us. I hear he rested his men at the Tate plantation, but now our scouts have lost his trail. I feel we must engage them soon or not at all.

I recall the same expectation of battle back in '46 on the long road that led from Stirling to Inverness. The Jacobite army said good-bye to the Lowlands on the first day of February that year. We headed for the Ford of Frew in small bodies, our carts overturned and left behind. This made a bad appearance, as though we had been routed in battle. A night in Dunblane, which my father recalled from the "Fifteen," and then we pressed on to Crieff, where a review of the army was held. It showed us to be more of a force than some had feared. To make foraging easier in the wintery land we divided into two parties. The prince led us Highlanders over Wade's military road, while Lord George took the Lowland regiments around the coast. Come spring, we were all to rendezvous at Inverness.

That was a hungry march, let me tell you. We went to

84

Taybridge and then to Dalnacardoch, where we met Lord Lewis Gordon with baggage and artillery from Perth. He brought us no food to speak of, and the less I had the more I dreamed of it—first of a slab of beef or venison, but as the long year wound down I conjured up anything with an honest taste. I kept thinking of a raw onion, or a potato fresh from the ground.

The snow fell and melted, and fell and melted, until it finally fell and clung, so that the farmhouses along the way wore hats and eyebrows. It looked very pretty, but we had to halt a few days at Blair again because of the hard going. I had icicles in my eyebrows when we got there, and it felt as if snow had drifted into my brain. My head seemed frozen solid, and only my chattering teeth were lively.

After Blair we strung out along the road to forage. Our band of Glencoe MacDonalds would have been smaller by half if we'd been nearer home. It wouldn't have taken much for me to desert old Charlie then, and I told my father so.

"Aye, lad, I'd sooner be sitting beside the fire at home, and you must do what you think right. I know you're a true MacDonald and will do that." His voice had a cough waiting in it. "So away with you. Who knows, it may be better." Then he rocked back and forth as his cough took over, and we spoke no more on the subject.

Of course I stayed on, to the bitter end and after, but it wasn't honor or loyalty that held me so much as fear of the Grampians alone, and all those other mountains between me and home, where winter prowled the high passes like a hungry wolf.

There was no use my talking to Angus Og, for he had heard the hated Campbells were a part of Cumberland's army, and he seemed only to yearn for the time of reckoning.

Meanwhile, we reduced the government fort at Ruthven,

but its stores offered little by way of food or comfort for our men. We heard that Lord George had snow aplenty as he followed the coast road. The idea was that he'd keep the road and the ports open for the French, who kept leaking reports that several of their regiments were about to sail for Scotland. This was the same old story, and few of us had any faith in the French at this point. Morale was low. We won battle after battle and still seemed to be losing the war. Could a cause be lost when it was believed in by men like Lord George and the prince? I began to think so, for with our hands full of victories we'd soon die of starvation and the elements. As Sir Thomas Sheridan wrote after Falkirk, "We are indeed like the old man who said, 'I am feeling very well, thank God, but I am going to die soon.' "

Despite our troubles, the prince's spirits seemed revived and he rode among us on horseback. Though I did not encounter him myself, it was hinted his high spirits came from a bottle. He no longer marched with us on foot, or spoke with the men, but mixed only with the likes of O'Sullivan and those who had come with him from the continent.

After nearly three weeks of marching we approached Inverness, the capital of the Highlands, and a shabby place it seemed, with dirty, windowless turf-faced hovels and the muddy streets full of refuse. In the center of town were a few red sandstone houses with stepped gables, with nary a window on the ground floor. At our coming the government garrison under Lord Loudon fled across the firth by the Kessock ferry, and Fort George gave up without much of a fight.

Only a few of us were quartered in the town. The army, what was left of it, set up camp on the bare moors to the east, the territory of that confederation known as Clan Chattan, who were MacKintoshes for the most part, MacPhersons, and others.

Meanwhile there were rumors of Cumberland. We'd out-run him, for what that was worth, having passed through Blair when he was only marching into Perth. He gave up our pursuit as hopeless and quartered his army for the winter at Aberdeen. It was said Cumberland thought Prince Charles would leave us and return to France, as his father James had done in '15.

I'd begun to have doubts about Charlie ever since Derby, where perhaps he'd begun to have doubts about himself. Now, outside Inverness, he set up in fair style at Culloden House, where he and his French cronies did considerable hunting, fishing, and dancing, and took no part in the sieges that were being won and lost. I began to wonder if the prince had come to give us freedom and a bright future, or to take our loyalty and our lives for his vanity. I still don't have the answer, and in those days I was too busy chopping sticks with my sword and foraging for any dry old loose-skinned apple to dwell upon it. Officially, our ration was down to one flour-and-water biscuit a day. The war chest was empty, and the farmers gave out no more victuals than money or force could extract. There was grumbling aplenty, not so much against the prince as against the Frenchies who surrounded him.

Although we were well behind the so-called Highland line, the real mountains as I knew them lay in the west, still snowclad and becoming an appeal that was answered by many whose homes were not far away. Around us the moors sloped gently to the firth and eastward toward Aberdeen, whence Cumberland would come with the spring. It was not land to suit a Highland warrior, and Angus Og, when he was not talking about being wed to my sister Mary in the summer, to which Father had long given his pleased consent, insisted we should withdraw into the real mountains. Most of the men would gladly have done so, but

Inverness was Charlie's last capital and the last port where the French fleet might appear, and so the prince clung to it. With the earth drying out and the first sign of spring growth, he sent out scurriers to call back our scattered bands so that we might boldly march upon Aberdeen.

Clearly my father did not rejoice, but he seemed resigned. "If your mother were here," he said, "she would tell us that Fate had chosen this place centuries ago. But I wonder, is that how things work? Our Charlie reckons he has God tucked away in his sporran, and up to now he's had the odds. No more, from what I hear. But knowing our Charlie, he'll go right ahead when he has only a hundred men to do the work of thousands. Then perhaps he'll discover God's only on the side of the big regiments. All I know is, 'tis a poor mean land for eating and for fighting, and that's the way of it." My father spent much time darkly brooding, and his cough would not go away. It was from feeling so down, I'm sure, that he suggested I go home with messages.

"And not return?"

"Aye, stay and guard the place. I fear for the women, and the stock as well," but I sensed he feared for me as well. Certainly he would not have the ladies visiting again. "Much too far," he said, but I still believe it wasn't the miles but Cumberland he dreaded.

We came to no agreement that evening, and all I did was write a letter home when I might have gone instead, passing my loneliness along if anyone could be found to make the delivery. Then I lay down to sleep. My freezing fingers found their way inside my plaid and I pressed them against my aching belly, where hunger had been for many days. The rain drilled on the roof of the old shed like nails being pounded into rotten wood. That dark glittery night brought back the fear, and I dreamed of the Bean Nighe, that old washerwoman who laundered the shrouds of the dead by night, and I dreamed the shroud was mine.

In the morning my father said as though in jest that if I decided to go home, I might bring back an honest meal all around. But he did not press me further, and before all our men were called back, word came that Cumberland was moving. On the twelfth day of April he had crossed the River Spey and was marching on Nairn, just half a day's walk away from us.

All sorts of rumors and reports preceded Cumberland's army: that they were hardened veterans of the continental wars trained in special new tactics designed to turn our charge, such as metal skullcaps to deflect our broadsword blades. But all that mattered to Angus Og was that Camp-bells were among them. He sharpened his sword painstak-ingly and had me do the same while my father watched us. He spoke not of home but said grimly, "I am no coward, but if you were to ask I would say, there are many alive this day who will be dead before the week is spent."

Angus ran an appraising finger along the edge of his sword, down one side and back the other. How confounded he would be today if he were aware I followed a Campbell toward yet another desperate battle.

It was strange, then, how the government army seemed to vanish and the rumors became stale old news, until a clear April morning when there came hail and sunshine both together. We were mustered and drawn up that day on Drummossie Moor near Culloden House as though the enemy were upon us. All there was to strengthen our bodies were a few loaves of bannock, that coarse bread made of the oat husks and sweepings from the mill floor.

We waited, and nothing more happened. We were dis-missed, to grind our teeth on the bannock. Then the word went around that Cumberland was celebrating his birthday at Nairn, and his soldiers were swilling down brandy and great chunks of cheese. Our mouths watered from the telling, and we made fun of Cumberland the fat, the overfed. He was yet to earn his more lasting nickname, "The Butcher." All such tomfoolery was forgotten that afternoon when we learned we would march at dusk, to fall upon the enemy before they could sleep off their celebrations. With any luck the war would be triumphantly concluded before dawn.

# 11

*North Carolina*
*The farm of Peter Quinn*
OCTOBER 5, 1780

It has been raining. Once again we have tried to pursue our foe by night, and once again we have lost our way, but this time we have food in our saddlebags and warm blankets, and our rifles are well wrapped against the wet.

Back in '46 we had no such luxuries, but it was hoped the duke of Cumberland's army might be drunk from celebrating his birthday, and Prince Charles delighted in Lord George's scheme to fall on the duke's camp outside Nairn.

We had eight miles to cover before the sun rose and many of our men were off foraging, so we did not get under way until after dark. Lord George led the first column of Highlanders and the prince brought up the rear. The MacKintoshes, whose land this was, were our guides, but the paths seemed trackless and deep in mud. There was many a quarrel about which way to go. The moon emerged before us, a sad grin in the sky, which quickly hid behind tattered clouds. Gnarled tree roots caused our feet to stumble, and with every step in that soft carpet of dead leaves, mud oozed up, trying to hold us fast.

We MacDonalds went blindly, having no idea of the route to Nairn, shuffling along single file, often with a hand upon the shoulder of the man ahead. I heard strange sounds and wondered if they were made by our own men or by the shifting of some strong ghost that haunted the land.

The only chance for our success was surprise, but as the night wore on we became too exhausted for stealth. I caught up with my father, who leaned against a tree. He was tired, too. "We're near them," he said. "We must be."

Our task, under Lord George's direction, was to attack Cumberland's encampment from the south, overturning the tents and striking any bulge that appeared in the canvas. The prince's men would charge in from the east. But there were already traces of dawn in the sky when the Mac-Kintosh scouts reported spotting Cumberland's camp. It seemed to me we should have to strike at once, but there was a delay while Lord George conferred with his officers. The sky grew paler as the sun rose, though all was gray. From Cumberland's camp we heard the *tum-tum-tum* of the call to arms, and then there rose plumes of white smoke. The butchers were burning their garbage, and my stomach turned at the thought of an army with red meat and garbage to squander.

A cannon fired from the artillery park, then another, the thuds muffled in the damp air. We were clearly discovered, but when the squeal of pipes joined in the noise, Angus said "Campbells!" and would have instantly attacked. He would not have been alone.

Not only had we not taken them by surprise, but the prince's column had fallen well behind the rest of us. Lord George turned us about, and we were trudging back toward Culloden Moor when Charlie galloped by. He reined in, and I saw his face red and bloated and doubted not the tales of his drunkeness.

"Where the devil are you men going?" he shouted. "What is the need of my giving orders when I'm always disobeyed?" He rolled his china-blue outraged eyes. "I am betrayed." His horse, an arthritic old gelding, pranced in nervous circles and we all gave ground, fearful of the man, who seemed insane. Then Lochiel and another officer—I think it was Perth—grabbed hold of his bridle. "You wicked men!" he shouted at them. "If your counsel were of God, He would not deliver you!" But even Charlie could not resist their steering, and his head slumped forward as he went off.

"Drunk as usual," said Angus, who never did give Charlie the benefit of the doubt. Drunk or not, the prince was soon riding among us again and under good self-control. "There's no help for it, my lads. We must march back," he shouted. "No doubt we'll meet them soon, and fight like brave fellows."

The sun rode low behind us over the moorland, throwing our shadows far ahead like spears. Those slanting rays were cold as the moon's, and just as cheerless. It was all I could do to plant one foot after another. A good many swords and targets had been cast aside on that failed and fruitless march, and I could have used a target on the day that was to be the worst in my life, but I was too tired for the added burden. I have never been so tired. I doubt I'll ever be so tired again until the day I die.

For the most part the officers staggered off to Culloden House and threw themselves down on feather beds. The rest of us had naught but the thickets, occasional empty sheds and barns on the moor there, but I was so spent I felt sick, and when I found a wee barn, though it was full of men, I fell down upon a patch of straw, thinking just so long as trouble does not come today. Sleep struck me down like a weapon, yet I dreamed of the red English ranks. In my dream they were unbelievably tall, with inhuman yellow eyes, which glinted a glare of deadly delight.

Hardly had sleep arrived, or so it seemed, than drums beat in my slumber. Then the thud of cannon aroused me. It was the recall. Many never heard it, or feigned so, but in our small barn the MacDonalds of Glencoe pulled themselves together slowly and fretfully, as men will who can scarce overcome their exhaustion.

I stepped outside and had to shade my eyes. It was a pleasant bright spring morn. From far off came the skirl of massed pipes.

"Are they volunteers coming in?" I ventured, always the optimist.

"Campbells, more likely," was Angus Og's dour reply.

Standing on the moor of Culloden and facing toward Nairn, from whence the piping came, the River Ness and the mountains of the Highlands were behind us, with the River Nairn off to the left and the widening firth and the parks of Culloden House on the right. Overhead the pleasant skies were thickening, and clouds swollen and bruised-looking sailed from the northeast. A solitary sea gull floated on motionless wings, giving weird and restless cries. It seemed a harbinger of ill omen, and my skin crawled. Always before a battle soldiers talk of having premonitions of death, and often when someone is killed it seems he had told of his expectations, but I had premonitions on every such morning.

Though our enemy was not yet in sight, as far as I could see the clans were forming a line, along which Prince Charles rode on his gray gelding. There was a cockaded bonnet on his head, a tartan jacket on his back, and a slender broadsword by his side. He kept shouting in that lisping

Italian accent of his, "Come on, my lads! This day will be ours!" at which cheers went up and bonnets were raised.

I was no tactician, but I looked around, thinking, Well, I reckon it's going to be here. My father stood long and said finally, "Lord, 'tis a terrible place for Highlanders." I later learned the ground had been selected by O'Sullivan over Lord George's urging that we withdraw to the rougher ground before Dalcross Castle, which would be harder for the English horse and artillery to cross. Charlie was said to have raged and damned them all, more angry with his disobedient Scots than with the enemy. He sided with O'Sullivan, presuming that God would have the final say regardless of where we fought. There was no denying this was Prince Charlie's day.

So the clans—those that could be called back from foraging or roused from exhausted sleep—lined up on Culloden Moor. Lord George, sensing doom upon the day, asked only that he command his Atholl men upon the right flank. Then came Camerons, Stewarts of Appin, Farquharsons, MacLeans, MacLachlans, MacKintoshes, Frasers. I have but a rough idea of how we were disposed. The duke of Perth had charge of the left flank, mostly the MacDonalds of Clanranald, Glengarry, and Keppoch. As a small clan, we were attached to the Keppoch regiment, three hundred strong. Sensing the discontent of many, the duke of Perth came by, his bonnet lifted courteously, to assure us. "If you fight with your usual bravery you will make the left wing a right wing today." Courageous words don't always turn the tide. The prince rode among us also, like a child living an adventure. He waved his sword and pointed to my own drawn blade and shouted, "I'll wager that will cut off some heads and arms this day!"

The morning had nearly spent itself when the moor to the east began to darken. I was perplexed at first, as though

95

it were a cloud shadow, yet all was in shadow now. Then I realized it was the enemy arriving in three columns, becoming a scarlet-and-white wall. There were the pipers and the *rat-tat* of kettle drums. Grenadier drummers of the Royal Scots came on with their sticks poised as high as their tall caps, then brought them down. Sixteen battalions of infantry advanced with a slow and methodical tread, another battalion of militia, three regiments of horse, and the company of artillery. Even Angus had to admire their symmetry as he put a final edge on his blade. One after another they wheeled into line, company after company, moving half right through a quarter circle with their sergeants bawling, "Dress, close steps!"

Between the battalions two three-pounders were manhandled to the front by gunners in blue coats. Before each battalion, flags were stationed. When the sun poked hazily through the even row, shouldered bayonets sparkled like a picket fence. Despite being over a quarter-mile distant, the enemy looked big and strong and well fed, and for each one of us who stood there I reckoned there were three of them, so confident of victory that they let their wives ride up in coaches to see the sport as they'd watch a fox hunt back home.

There was an odd, respectful silence in our ranks as we watched the enemy showing off, and a bitter smell that I had come to know. A good soldier may take command of his speech and expression, but not that faint odor of fear, nor the little drops of sweat that appear on forehead and upper lip. My father kept his feelings under control like a determined, clench-jawed rider guiding a panicked horse, and I knew he'd be happier with me well back in the support line, the place for boys and old men, unhorsed cavalry, and Lowlanders who, at Prestonpans, had been described as having stood stock still like oxen. But in this argument he'd lost conviction.

"Colin, there is much of Judgment Day about this dreary moor. Would you not be sensible, and step back with the lads your age? Be sensible, for your mother's sake. 'Twill reflect no discredit on you." And if that wasn't enough: "Think of Peggy Sinclair. Be sensible, lad."

But I was a fool like the rest of them, or I would not have been there in the first place, and I still almost have to laugh when I think of the fond and foolish thing my father was about to do, and him talking solemnly of good sense. Then Glenaladale's piper struck up "Hey, Johnnie Cope," and Father was obliged to stick his own chanter between his lips, and our talk was done.

> Cope sent a letter from Dunbar
> Saying, "Charlie, meet me if ye daur
> And I'll learn you the art of war,
> Right early in the morning."

I sang along as did others, and the gloomy mood seemed to lift, though it never did banish the deep discontent of some of our clan for being deprived of the traditional right flank. To me this seemed foolish—you can kill or be killed anywhere up and down the front line in a battle—but it meant a lot to the MacDonald veterans, and certainly it played a part in what was about to happen.

I reckon it was well past noon when things got started. By now the weather had cleared a bit, but the wind still blew in our faces. Seems like if God had been on our side, like Charlie supposed, it would have swung right around with a bit of rain to boot, as it did at Falkirk.

When an English officer rode out between the lines bold as brass, someone fired on him. It missed, but he rode on calm as could be. We pumped up a thin cheer from exhausted lungs, and the English gave us back a short hoarse hurrah.

Nothing really had happened. Still, we know it was building up. Everyone sensed it, and some began singing the twentieth Psalm. Then the different clan pipers picked up on the rant and drowned out our voices. Finally a four-gun battery toward the center of our line opened fire, too slow and erratic to interfere with the sound of the pipes. A few minutes later Cumberland's cannoneers replied, and I could see the guns jumping as if they'd been struck by whips. The blue-coated gunners sprang to reload. Down the line, a man fell and rolled flat. It was all so calm, except for the cannon and the distant shaking of the earth.

By now the sky, which had been steely gray, took on a sulfurous yellow from the smoke blowing from the English cannon. Our own guns quickly fell silent, leaving only the pipes to cheer us on while the English three-pounders kept booming. Sometimes I could hear their bombardiers yelling, "Sponge!" and then, "Powder! . . . Ram! . . . Load! . . . Ready! . . . Fire!" with the smoke rolling and tumbling over the ground to tear away, blue-gray and yellow, blinding us. I'll tell you, it was infuriating to see the immunity of those guns as they pounded us. No order to advance was given, so all any of us could do was wave our swords and curse.

Reality had departed. I was groggy and excited both at once. My feet didn't seem to touch solid ground, but the craziness of it all really took over when my father reached out and parried a cannonball that came bounding our way with his sword. "Look out, Colin!" he shouted, and I leaped aside, though the ball had about spent itself. Still, it had enough force to run along his blade and into the guard, throwing Father down. At first I thought he was joking.

His lips formed as though to whistle, but no sound came. Then I saw how the sword dangled from his arm and realized his wrist was broken. What a fool thing to do, though I can't say that or even think it, for he'd acted out of concern for me.

Cursing himself for an idiot, my father got to his feet with my help and painfully resheathed the old family sword with his left hand. The sword's basket was crumpled out of all recognition. His pipes were slung on his back, but he could not play them, either. The battle of Culloden Moor was scarcely begun, yet for my father it was finished. All he could do was go wincing to the rear.

The rest of us stood our ground and cringed as the cannon thinned our already depleted ranks, waiting for the prince's command to charge. Some lay flat, others fled. It was an awful nightmare. From a slope behind the right wing, the prince looked on. Though I was told Lord George and the other chiefs pleaded for a general advance, a half-hour went by and still no order arrived.

I later learned it was Donald, the "Gentle Lochiel," who could hold his Camerons no longer. With a roar they rushed to attack, and the right side of the line broke with them: Lord George amid his Atholl men, the Stewarts of Appin, MacKintoshes, MacBeans, the men of Clan Chattan led by the yellow-haired Dunmaglas and his standard-bearer. MacGillivrays bounded into the smoke as well, shouting "Loch Moy!" and "Dunmaglas!" and shafts of yellow lightning stabbed at them and they leaned into the grapeshot as though it were hail. At last they must have seen a row of white-gaitered legs and then the bright spittings of the muskets firing in sequence, front rank, second, and finally third. Some crashed through the first row of bayonets. Too proud to retreat, others stood before the fire, throwing stones until they fell. For a moment, word came that the

Camerons had broken through. Barrell's regiment and Munro's were said to be in flight. We sent up a cheer, but it did not last. The British had been taught a new way of fighting our swords and targets—by striking low, and at the man to their right, thereby avoiding our best defense. It was a slaughter.

The rest of our line stood like men bound to stakes. We'd had no orders, and when the MacLachlans and Mac-Kintoshes bolted forward, our flank was left open to the enemy. Finally, Colonel MacGillivray of Dunmaglas moved ahead with the center of our line. Then Keppoch stepped out before his men, his sword drawn, and shouted, "Oh, my God, has it come to this, that the children of my tribe have forsaken me?" He and his brother Donald went on toward the enemy, never looking back. Donald fell first, then Keppoch, who rose not once but twice before he lay down for good.

I'm ashamed to admit that many of our officers and chiefs fell and no MacDonald clansmen followed. By now the Camerons and Atholl men were staggering back out of the smoke, and not even Lord George could hold them.

Suddenly Angus Og Sinclair drew his blade, the tip black from toasting potatoes, and bounded forward. With my father gone, I helplessly followed Angus as my legs bore me where the rest of me dared not go, toward that wall of boiling smoke slashed by bladelike fires.

I saw Angus disappear into that devouring cloud. There must have been a terrible fury upon him, for he hewed his way through the bayonets as far as any MacDonald, officer or man, did go, and then he was returning carefully, as though his body was brittle. Standing before me, he said, "Colin?" as though he wasn't sure. Then he fell, to lie at my feet like a bundle of old clothes.

The assault went no further. The battle of Culloden was

virtually over, though I did not know it. My whole concern was for Angus. He looked to be dead, but I heard myself pleading, "Angus, are you all right?" and I held his hand and felt his forehead.

"I don't know," he said, and shook his head back and forth, his lips clamped tight. Somehow I lugged him to his feet and we made slow progress, with his sword hanging down between his legs like a dog's beaten tail. It was only then I realized my own sword had vanished, that fine MacGregor blade. There was no going back for it, and that was just as well. Its loss may well have saved my life before the day was done.

The flight was on, all up and down the line. Lord George flung his pistols at his fleeing men, he struck them with the flat of his sword, he pleaded, commanded, and threatened at the top of his lungs, but they were running now. He was one of a handful of officers to survive the fire of the Campbells, who came on with their triumphant cry, "Cruachan!"

The prince, too, tried to rally his army back in a suicidal charge. For a moment, as I paused to rest with Angus slumped on my shoulder, the prince's horse reared before me. In a flash the air seemed full of striking hooves, and then Lochiel's uncle, Major Kennedy, took hold of Charlie's horse's bridle. Such was the prince's fate, always to be led off against his will.

O'Sullivan, that master tactician, groaning that all was lost, also caught hold of his bridle. All around Charlie were his French supporters. They had filled his ears with evil rumors that we Highlanders would betray him for his gold, though I believe he resisted them at first. Now Charlie sagged in his saddle, his face wet with tears and his sword drooping in loose fingers. God knows, death in the fray might have been a judgment of mercy for a prince whose cause was lost, but I'm not sure Charlie ever arrived at such a realization. In any case, he let them draw him off to safety, away from his men who were dead or dying. Only then did Lord Elcho call after him bitterly, "Run away, you cowardly Italian!"

Though our paths would cross one last time, just then Charlie was no concern of mine. I had Angus to worry about. He did not speak but clung silently to me like a baby being carried half asleep to its bed, too weary for further protest. Though he was losing more and more blood, he seemed to become heavier at each step.

The best I could do was to drag Angus inside a small shed not far behind the battlefield. There were other wounded men there already, and he lay among them like a hammer-struck steer, not knowing whether he was alive or dead. I lay beside him in the straw, whispering the Act of Contrition for us both, "Oh, my God, I am heartily sorry for having offended Thee," over and over, for those were all the words I could recall.

Angus lay with his hands pressed against his wound, as though he might keep life from leaking out. "I'm cold," he said, his eyes as dull as dry pebbles. "I'm freezing." I took off my plaid and covered him. "We'll get help," I said. "You'll be fine." He shook his head, and I grasped his hand. He clung to me like a bairn afraid to be left alone in the dark, and his breathing was all shudders and gurgles. In the corner, another man screamed at intervals, loudly and without shame. I think he'd been shot in the belly.

It may have been those screams that brought the enemy. I suppose someone would have found us in the end, but perhaps it would not have been Campbells.

Seeing the kilts, I thought at first it meant help, but Diarmid's badge of myrtle and the red saltire showed their allegiance to King George. I might have covered Angus with straw or lain on top of him myself, but I'll not deny I stayed where I was, cringing with fear while the Campbells went around with their swords and bayonets, doing what time would surely have done to the wounded there. A sword was raised above me, and I crouched down whimpering and cradled my head in my arms, waiting for the blow. It never came.

"It's just a lad, unarmed at that," one of them said.

"Who'd grow up to knife us in the back, by and by." There was more truth in this than any of us knew.

" 'Tis a bloody day. Leave the lad be."

And with that they trudged out. Angus still lay beside me, his arms flung wide and his head dangling backward. If blood had not oozed from his mouth, I would have thought he was asleep. He looked so peaceful I almost envied him.

For a long time I lay there, until I was sure dusk had come. Little by little I felt Angus turning cold, and I asked for nothing save that he might be alive somehow. Finally, I said a prayer for his soul and twined a small cross that he carried into his fingers. Then I prepared to leave, fearing the Campbells or other soldiers might appear. The rest of the night I spent hidden in a nearby blackberry thicket, for it seemed only fitting to bury Angus come morning, but when I awoke the shed where he lay was engulfed in flames, and I saw redcoats carrying torches.

For all I knew, I was the only Jacobite left alive, and I crawled off through the brambles and heather, with the terror of probing bayonets always behind me.

It was not until days later that the closing events of that desperate day filled out in my mind. Lord George had kept the right wing together in orderly retreat, and the Irish Picquets had made a gallant stand behind the boundary wall of the Black Park, but the rest of the army had made

103

off in panic down the road to Inverness with Kingston's horse in hot pursuit, cutting them down at will. Many good Samaritans, come to succor the wounded, were cut down for their trouble, and so were those of low character seeking booty.

Before sunset Cumberland, at the head of a captain's guard of dragoons, with sword in hand, scarlet coat mud spattered, and his chubby face shiny with sweat, rode into Inverness. The bells that had rung weeks before for Charlie now rang for him. On the firth, the guns of his supply ships boomed in victory.

I dared not follow the road but clung to the moor, heading southwest toward the River Ness and home. Only once did I look back. The shed was still red but it had sunk down, and little red flakes swirled upward into the sky. Soon there would be no trace of it, and Angus Og would lie forever on the moor, with the passing seasons making a clean white chapel of his bones.

# 12

I'd not go into the rest, for it does no one any credit, but 'tis a part of my story and as important a part of Charlie's Year as any other. I was alone and trying to put a distance between myself and King George's army, though a great many other fugitives shared my fate. Cumberland had taken over Inverness, and the townspeople had turned their backs on us. What else could they do? A few Jacobites tried to sneak through and some succeeded, but most were stopped by sentries who turned them in to the authorities or accepted bribes to let them go, according to their natures.

I kept well away from the town and headed south. After a few miles I met up with two of our men whom I recognized, and they said some of our army would muster yet again at Ruthven Barracks, though they had heard the prince was already on his way to France to raise gold and soldiers. I had naught in my belly but two biscuits and I felt shaky and lightheaded, else I'd have headed straight for my old home. I'd had my fill of heroes and heroics, but men and boys are creatures of habit, and as the number of our fleeing men grew, I stumbled along with the crowd. There was much grumbling and the usual rumors about the prince. Many were sure he'd left Scotland forever, and the talk was bitter. They were wrong, of course. I was to rue the day he entered my life again.

I did have one bit of luck on the way south to Ruthven Barracks, for I ran into a troop of Glencoe MacDonalds, and limping along with them was my father. Needless to say, our reunion was a surprise and a delight, though he looked very much the worse for wear. His right arm was done up in a dirty sling, and he looked very thin and gray as sin. Still he brightened up in the old way when he saw me. "You've a stout heart and that's a fact," he said. I exclaimed over his appearance, and he said, "Och, I'm fine, laddie." But he was far from fine, and he looked worse still at the sad news of Angus Og Sinclair, who had become as much a son to him as he had been an older brother to me.

After heading south down the Great Glen, we turned east for Ruthven Barracks, which still harbored a goodly host of Highland officers. The duke of Perth and his brother, Lord John, were there, along with Lord Ogilvie, but the most important to us was our Lord George Murray. All of them awaited instructions from the prince. If he had chosen to ask, the Camerons, Glenronalds, and the men of Glenmoriston would have rallied to his cause, but others, including the men of Keppoch, with whom we had fought, would have refused. Many clansmen never declared themselves one way or the other, but it never came to issue among them. Charlie settled all that with his message: "Let every man seek his own safety the best way he can." Evidently he thought he was off directly to France, and some said, What could you expect of a coward with a price on his head? He'd have been a dead man if he'd been caught in Scotland. There was a Roderick MacKenzie who was mistaken for our Charlie, and the English soldiers cut his head off on the spot. I'd learned the prince wasn't perfect, but I still say he was no coward, and he was abused worse than he deserved in those stone buildings at Ruthven. But then we were beaten and bitter men, needing someone to blame.

Lord George had the last word, which was fitting: "You men have fought bravely. We are all comrades in arms, and I thank you for all the dark days with me. Now the sun's gone down and willna rise again in our lifetime."

"Say ye so?" someone asked in disbelief.

And after a pause Lord George said, "Aye, 'tis the way of it. As the prince said, you've done your duty. Now's the time for each of you to fend for yourselves." Then he turned and walked out and, I gather, was in Europe before my father and I had found our way back to the Great Glen.

We went slowly, off the beaten path when we could, for the enemy was abroad and laying waste to the land as we had never done to them. My father said it would stop once the fury of battle had passed, but he was wrong. Meanwhile, we clung to the hills, passing through ravines of gray and scarlet stone, seeing naught but an occasional red deer among the pines and eagles soaring above the summits still capped with snow.

My father's health was worse than I'd realized. It all showed in his face, which was drawn and grim, and in the way he moved, as though there was dry sand in his joints. He had begun to limp, raising one shoulder higher than the other, and often he went with a hand on my shoulder.

The night after we rounded Ben Alder he said, "I hurt too much to be dead," then he pulled his plaid over him and slept face down in the heather with his arms out to the sides. Those were dark nights without mortal-made light, and though I kept watch for the quick and the dead I saw neither in the wilds. Toward dawn the leaves shook down their dew upon us and set us on our way.

Under the snow-laden ridges of the Great Glen we sometimes heard the sound of drums. May was a month of rebel hunting there, and three battalions of the king's army had marched down from Inverness to Fort Augustus, with the Campbells out as scouts. This was no battle fury, but a policy dictated in high places, with which they meant to crush the clans forever. Our banners, seized at Culloden, were burned by the hangman of Edinburgh before the market cross, and a good many chiefs, to avoid prosecution, brought in their weapons. Others, expecting pardon, tried to do so, only to be hung naked, their clothes going to the executioner. Simply to tend the wounds of a Jacobite meant that one's house could be burned, and throughout that long summer of '46 there lingered on the air the faint smell of smoke.

Cumberland did not lack for men to hound us. Twenty infantry battalions were at his disposal, not to mention three cavalry regiments, a goodly supply of Hessians and Campbells, as well as Admiral Byng's sloops of war. In some villages the government troops were received with courtesy. Other villages were abandoned by their dwellers when they heard the sound of drums, in which case they were looted and often burned as well, on principle. When the troops had time they took great houses apart. The slates from the roofs, the timbers from the frames, and even the nails were collected and sold. Almost no one fought back, for there was a great numbing shock of defeat and hunger upon the land, and those who had marched home from Culloden with weapons brandished, like the MacGregors, were promptly visited by the troops.

We were not the first survivors of the prince's cause to straggle home to Glencoe that spring of '46, nor the last. The women were already accustomed to tearing their kerchiefs into bandages when they saw us coming.

My mother appeared in the doorway as we trudged up the last few yards, and I was so tired I nearly cried, just knowing I was home at last. She took my hands in hers without turning her gaze from my face, and her stern eyes, though more imperious than ever, were full of tears. Realizing that I was intact, she dismissed me with, "You're taller, Colin. Yes, you've thinned out a good deal." She turned on my father. "But just look at this old fool. What's happened to him?"

She fed us broth and fresh oatcakes and cheese for supper, and though I ate quickly I recall to this day the taste of that wholesome food. My father was so exhausted by the time he finished he needed help getting to bed. The last words he spoke were said as a joke but more close to true. "Don't wake me in the morning, Elspeth. I may be dead." That reminded me of Angus Og, and I asked about Mary, who was still tending the cattle. She came in just as darkness fell, and I think she must have had some of mother's gift for knowing in advance, for her first words were, "Angus is dead, isn't he?" It was not a question, and I just looked at her. Her hands had gone to either side of her face. In times of trial Mary was among the dignified ones. Most women seem to find relief in tears, but not my sister. Her features tightened, but nary a muscle moved after that. When I embraced her, her body was rigid in my arms.

I told her the story once, and what I told was a lie. I made Angus Og a hero, and he was that, but I got his dying over with in the thick of the fight, quickly and painlessly as some believe it can be when death comes in hot blood. Mary never asked me about it again, never spoke of her lost love. She even seemed her old self, though ever after her laughter has haunted me, and deep down I think sadness enveloped her like a shroud. Never did she complain, only went on keeping the black cattle, wandering through the ravines and valleys like a cloud shadow. She sang to them when she was alone, and there are stories still of the singing. Later, she talked to the cattle and to herself.

# 13

*Cowpens*

OCTOBER 6, 1780

The weather bodes ill. We patriot volunteers, whom some call rebels, are now nearly eighteen hundred strong. We have learned that our foe, Major Patrick Ferguson and his legion, are but a few miles hence at Peter Quinn's place and about to withdraw a further six miles to Kings Mountain, there to await reinforcements from General Cornwallis. 'Tis a remote and rough countryside ahead that reminds me of the high hills south of Glencoe whence we fled with the black cattle during the summer of '46.

Many families from the Glen withdrew on foot or galloway when the militia marched up from Fort William. There were caves up there, and morning mist. The birch and pine grew thick and tall, and it was a bonnie place to hide. Some folk buried their silver and other valuables, but most of us had none to hide. So there was less looting and burning in Glencoe than elsewhere, though I did hear that the chief's old cook was shot for not revealing the hiding place of the family's treasure.

Where we climbed with the herd was once the abode of

long-haired Gingalian giants. Above Loch Achtriachtan is a vast cave where Ossian, the poet son of Fionn, composed heroic verse. The mountains there, five ridges in all, form a loosely clenched fist bound to the great knuckles of Didan nam Ban, the Pinnacle of the Peaks. There are no higher mountains in Argyll. We took Lairig Gartan, the green pass, through them to Glen Etive, and there, Mary promised, we would be safe. We patched up an old herdsman's shelter of rock and turf and settled down for the month of August. Mary knew it well from her wanderings with the cattle, and she showed me a place to stand on a thistled slope where a stream wandered down below. There you might sing aloud into this shell of bare rock scooped from the mountain wall, "Hey, Johnnie Cope, are you marching yet?" And right on cue the echo returned! "Marching yet, marching yet." Strange that I have never really marched, not in '45 or now, just trudged along with a mob of other tired men.

The prince's year was nearly unwound. It had a month to go, and though I would not have believed it standing with my sister in the wilderness, that month would count more in my life than all the months that had passed since his banner was first raised at Glenfinnan.

At this time there were many rumors about Charlie: He was trapped in the Outer Isles; he was already in France with his friend O'Sullivan, raising another army; he was dead. In truth, the fugitive prince had returned to the Highlands and was hiding deep in the wilds of Glenmoriston, mantained there by his supporters in a rebellion so thoroughly lost they were now called outlaws. Those eight men of Glenmoriston (numbered just seven by those who could not count) shall remain immortal for their loyalty and courage: Patrick Grant, Black Peter of Craskie, Alexander and John MacDonnell, the three brothers Hugh, Donald, and Alexander Chisholm, and Gregor MacGregor. They kept the prince hidden from the English patrols and led him southeast when the hunt closed on him.

We had no hint of this until a stranger came among us, the first human we had seen in a week, and with dark suspicion we stood around the man, who looked lean and dangerous with a brass-barreled blunderbuss crooked in his arm. "You had better know I've a dozen little lead friends in here," he said. "Every one of them can run faster than you can." We might have cast ourselves upon him all the same had he not added, "I'm looking for the famous piper, Cluny MacDonald. My name is Alexander MacPherson."

"Would you be kin to Benjamin MacPherson?" asked my father.

"Aye, I'm his son."

This eased the tension, and we all sat down, anxious to hear of the outside world. Alexander MacPherson had come looking for a guide to the saw-toothed land north of Glencoe. My father was the man he had in mind, but even a stranger could observe that he was unwell.

"I can do what must be," my father insisted, though his eyes seemed to be sitting on his cheekbones, and in his wasted face his nose had become very long.

MacPherson looked uncomfortable. "It will mean hard climbing, from east of here to the shores of Loch Linnhe."

"Aye, I know it well," my father said, and with many eyes upon him added, "I'm not so bashed as I look." But he was, and in the stillness of truth I heard Mary's voice volunteering. No doubt she knew all the paths hereabout.

"A wee lass?" said MacPherson.

Mary could have set a course as well as any man, but I heard my father volunteer my name. Under the circumstances, I could scarcely refuse. So it was toward the first of September 1746 that I found myself enlisted by a stranger to act as a guide through the mountains to a person or persons undisclosed. Having gotten me involved, my father was full of advice not to take unnecessary risks and to come straight home when the job was done. As a token and amulet of good luck, he presented me with his Rob Gib snuffbox. And so I took leave of my family, father, mother, and sister Mary, and if my heart felt slumped a bit off center it was more at the thought of hard traveling than from any sense I would never see any of them again.

Thus began the strangest interlude in my short life, hiking through the high country behind Alexander Mac-Pherson toward Ben Alder, where MacPherson of Cluny's cattle grazed still. Here the vegetation thinned and we passed upward through a steep slope full of sharp boulders.

"You're feeling it now, MacDonald," said my panting guide. "Lord knows, so am I." This was the abode of the eagle and the storm cloud. "Well, it's not far." By midafternoon he was pointing. "That's the place up ahead."

"I don't see it."

"You're not supposed to. 'Tis a secret lair. They call it Cluny's Cage."

We were nearing Ben Alder's final ridge. There in a rocky face, hidden by a grove of holly, was a cave, part natural and part man-made out of tree trunks and interwoven stakes. The smoke vent was so cleverly hidden among gray slabs of rock that a thin column of smoke was invisible.

Cluny MacPherson had fled here when patrols had burned his eighteen-room mansion. There was space inside the room of interwoven heath and birch twigs for half a dozen men. Yet only one was present when we arrived. He slumped at a table with his head upon his arms, a horn cup within reach of one hand and a small black pipe near the other. Disheveled, red-bearded, dirty and sunburned,

114

covered with scratches and the bites of midges and fleas, I knew this vagabond all the same.

I'm dead, I thought. My heart has stopped.

It was Prince Charles—all that was left of him. I could swear he'd been crying. His face was dirty in all the telltale places. Once we had entered he roused himself, confused at first, wearing the expression of a sleepy woman glimpsing her own powderless face in a looking glass. Then he laughed, puzzled. His mouth did not entirely close, then slowly his look of amazed bemusement gave way to the old friendly smile that was so hard to resist. "I know you," he said, and he seemed for all his wear and tear hardly less handsome than when I saw him first in all his glory. Yet something was gone. The light had faded. It was as though his eyes had clouded over.

Along with a handful of others, the prince and I shared Cluny's Cage for about a week, and during that time I formed certain impressions about Charlie. I'll not say I knew him as he had been before, or as he would be in future, but things were said and done, and I will put them down as memory serves, and let the reader draw his own conclusions.

I was introduced forthwith as his guide, in due course, to Loch Linnhe, and he said, "So this is Colin MacDonald. If I'd only had more men like you." He was gallantly smiling, as if to say, I will smile forever. "You see, MacDonald, I am in distress. I must throw myself onto your mercy. Do with me as you choose. I hear you are an honest man, and fit to be trusted." I scarcely knew how to reply. I'd just turned fifteen, and if he really wanted an army stocked with boys, he was a fool. If he did not, then he must think I was a fool. Yet he did have a winning way, and with a bleat of laughter he affectionately punched me on the shoulder. I cannot recall once during that week, despite his ill fortune, dysentery, and sores upon his legs and body from bad food and bug bites, that he did not remain generous and good spirited with those who shared his fate.

At times he seemed discouraged, but always he insisted his flight was a kind of providential trial. "Since Culloden," he confided, "I have endured more than would kill a hundred. Surely such a test is not for nothing. Recall that Robert the Bruce lost eleven battles and then snatched victory from defeat. Surely Fate has not brought me this far to perish in such circumstances. Surely it is meant that I undo the cruelties inflicted by Cumberland, and do some good work in this life."

The prince sometimes blamed the men who had served him in the past, particularly Lord George Murray, and this I must admit hurt me, for I retained a loyalty to Lord George. Often the prince played cards with the others, or sang loudly, tilting back in his chair and swaying his head to and fro, all the while drinking brandy. Starting a cork by striking the bottle with the heel of his hand, Charlie would draw the cork with his teeth, then spit it out and raise the bottle to his lips. Almost always he repeated the same words: "I have learned in my skulking to take a hearty dram." He would give a small gurgling laugh, and a bubble of brandy would form on his lower lip. He would hiccup, try to pretend he coughed, and after a tug at his red beard would say imploringly, "Please, Colin, talk to your friends and make them happy." The other card players would look reprovingly at him and then at each other.

He often talked to himself, made faces at his own answers, and when companions declined to drink, or he was alone, he drank and said, "I don't need this, I just like it." Or, "For what we are about to receive," and he'd drain the cup and then smack his lips. If I was there with a worried

116

look, he might contradict himself and say, "I need a little something these days to keep me going." I usually had no answer, and he might sight at me over the neck of the bottle as though over the barrel of a pistol. "Death or glory. Are you ready for that, lad, when I command?" And he would half wink for emphasis. "A cause to die for, Colin, my friend?"

"I'd prefer a cause to live for, sir," I told him once, feeling very bold.

"What if I told you my brother Henry was on his way from France with ten thousand men-at-arms? What if I said that to you?"

"I don't believe there's much hope, sir," I said very quietly, hoping he wouldn't hear me.

He rolled his heavy-lidded eyes heavenward. "Then you and I, Colin, shall have to go on without it. As for the English, I am not afraid of them. Let them clap me in irons!" And he joined his fists dramatically.

Alexander MacPherson came into our shelter at this moment and said, "Given the chance, Your Highness, they're more apt to shoot you on the spot."

"Very well, let them fire on me!" With this Charlie tore open his shirt and exposed an expanse of breastbone liberally speckled with the itch. His eyes flashed around as though we were tormenting a helpless animal. Then he stood up and backed away from the table, upsetting his stool. He weaved to the left, regained his balance, weaved to the right. Then he was on his way, going, going, gone. The entire cave reverberated. There followed a long silence. The half-empty bottle lay in the dirt beside him. His chin had sunk on his chest, and for a moment he glared up crookedly under his thick eyebrows with an expression compounding arrogance, confusion, and an uncertain sorrow. Then his eyes closed.

117

I must admit that although I felt sorrow for the prince and all the rest of us, I was losing my Stuart convictions. To lead others, it seems to me, one needs a certain quality of self-deception, and this our Charlie had in abundance; but a leader must have the strength of purpose to go first, and if Charlie were to do so it would be like a tallcase clock carried by the rest of us.

Seeing Scotland's hope lying there, I would happily have tiptoed out of the Cage and run all the way back to my family and the black cattle, but I had promised to serve as a guide, and to this purpose I had sworn a dread oath, that my back should be turned to God and my face to the Devil, that all the curses of Holy Scripture would descend upon me if I did not stand firm with my prince until he saw fit to release me.

We waited in Cluny's Cage for news of a ship. Sometimes there were alarms, as when the stones, absorbing the sun's heat, expanded with the crack of a pistol shot. Then we leaped up, thinking we were undone, but no one came until Alexander MacPherson returned with news of two French ships. *L'Heureux*, with thirty-six guns, and *Le Prince de Conti*, a thirty-two-gunner, had appeared in Loch Boisdale, flying English colors. How long they might linger undiscovered no one dared hazard, but with the dusk of that day decisions were made. At first the prince protested. Should he not stay and raise the western Highlands? I suspect he was playing a game, knowing full well that to stay was a death sentence. In the end, he complied. "I find kings and princes must be ruled by their privy council," he said graciously, "but I believe there is not in the world a more absolute privy council than what I have at present."

So we headed west that night, with the moon looking as thin and worn as an old silver coin. That the prince, immediately upon setting out, developed a nosebleed was a dark presentiment of what lay ahead.

Cluny MacPherson led the way at first, between Ben Alder and Loch Ericht, through Ben Alder forest, past the southern tip of Loch Laggan and into Glen Roy, going more north than south, so that I was never called on to lead the way and might have gone straight home for all the use I was as a guide.

We crossed the Great Glen north of Loch Linnhe, a good time to break off and visit the Sinclairs and their Peggy, but by then I was part of the expedition with a few chores to do in behalf of the prince and wanting to see him safe away. So I trudged along with the others as we went on remote deer trails between thick old trunks and gnarled, bulging roots where light scarcely found its way through the leaves, or over high ridges misted with cloud, until the sea lay below us, blue and pulsing with sunlight. It seemed more light than water.

The prince and I talked often in the course of those days on the road, and sometimes he spoke as though he were thinking aloud and thus shared a great many things with me. I was left with the impression that he felt he'd done a good deal for Scotland and would do more if Fate were kinder. It did not seem to cross his mind how much better off we all would have been if he had not come at all. Typical of our Charlie was a little episode involving Lochiel. Without Lochiel's support in the beginning, Lord knows if the rebellion ever would have gotten started. Then at Culloden, Lochiel was sorely wounded in both ankles, and on encountering the prince had tried painfully to go down on his knees. Charlie said, "Oh, no, my dear Lochiel." So far so good. But as he pulled poor Lochiel to his feet, he added, "You never know who may be watching from the tops of yonder hills."

119

The west coast of Scotland is not pretty, it's ferocious, and with frequent storms beating in from the North Atlantic upon hidden rocks and reefs, no ship is safe there for long, particularly a French warship awaiting a fugitive prince. But the weather held, and upon the pane of frosted glass that was Arisaig Sound two such ships anchored, a small forest of masts and rigging turning in their own inky reflections.

There, with the waves bursting upon the gray boulders and filling the small beach with the secret scrabble of pebbles sucked back in the dark undertow, Prince Charles took leave of those of us who chose not to accompany him back to France. Though he may well have been splitting in half with a hangover, he sustained the pose and manner of royalty to the end.

"I esteem you above other men," he informed us, "and trust one day I shall thank you for your trouble at St. James Palace. My lads, be of good spirits. It shall not be long before I shall be with you again, whereupon I will make good the losses you have suffered. There is money for the sustenance of the officers and to provide meals for all who are private men." I never saw food or money, but be that as it may, the prince was in good form. "May the Almighty bless and direct you." By now the sailors had set to their oars, and for good or bad our Charlie was gone from Scotland. It was the twentieth day of September 1746, and Prince Charlie's Year, *Bliadhna Thearlaich* in the Gaelic tongue, was finally and forever over.

About twenty-three gentlemen accompanied Charlie under the cover of the dawn mist: Lochiel, John Roy Stewart, and Dr. Archibald Cameron among them, and just over a hundred common folk. Over the still water I could hear him singing them aboard; they say ships always brought out the troubador in Charlie. By the time the sun rose the two ships were low on the horizon, and the wind that blew them out to sea was like a great sigh of relief from Scotland.

The rest of us who had fought for the prince and harbored him and were proud and loyal enough to ignore that vast reward that was never, in truth, collected began to disperse toward our homes. "Will Ye No Come Back Again?" was a song not yet composed, but had it been we would not have sung it then or later. All that any of us wanted was home, the patching up of lives so sorely interrupted by Charlie's Year. Autumn was in the air, and the oak and alder trees along the shore were yellow bands among the dark pines. There were brown shawls of bracken on the crests. Peggy was on my mind, and it occurred to me to visit the Sinclairs on my way home. But this was not to be.

Rain came and went as we broke up our camp. A gleam of sunshine through the curtains of rain reddened a nearby castle ruin and pricked out a figure that watched from the crumbling turret.

"Sassenach!" someone shouted, and so it was that we became prisoners.

Many had already left under cover of dark, but those who lingered, with a sad awareness that once we were gone the last Jacobite fellowship should be forever broken, were captured. No shots were fired, no blades drawn in that last stand by the murmuring tide. The government militia simply ringed us around with their overwhelming numbers, their muskets leveled, and we were led away. For us to resist and die there was more than Charlie deserved.

I have no intent to dwell on those dark months when I was a prisoner of the English, for it is a painful memory. Yet since it was a common reward for faithful Jacobites, I feel it requires some small attention. Long before Charlie had set sail for France, the trials of those who had garrisoned Carlisle began, and their leaders were dragged on

121

sledges to the gallows. After hanging, their still-breathing bodies were drawn and quartered and their hearts cast into a fire as the executioner shouted, "God save King George!" Their severed heads were raised on spikes above Fleet Street at Temple Bar in the City of London for all to see.

Such treatment was reserved for the more revered prisoners, though a man might be hung, without the trimmings, for singing a verse of "When the King Enjoys His Own Again." Most of us just languished in prison, on what was supposed to be a pound of bread a day. We seldom received half as much, and what appeared was full of weevils. For some time I and many others occupied the hold of a ship anchored off Inverness. Lying on my back I could see a patch of sky. There was nothing else to see, only the slowly changing colors as day became night and then day again. There were times when I thought as a free man and felt the desire to walk in the hills again. I could even hear the heather blowing around my feet, which made the damp and odorous hold of that old ship seem even more narrow, dark, and crowded. Sometimes they needed a quota for hanging, and we drew lots, with one in twenty receiving the black spot, which meant death. For the rest it was either pardon—rarely given—or transportation. It was my fate, along with many others, to be transported to the North American colonies.

Some prisoners were shipped out directly from Inverness, but my bad luck was to be sent to London first. Midway on the journey our ration of meal ran out, and a hundred or more died of starvation between Citadel Quay in Inverness and Thames Bank in London. I have seen that great city only through the portholes of a prison ship. I might have starved to death as well had it not been for my father's snuffbox, which caught the fancy of a guard. Its exchange brought me an extra portion now and then. I consumed this bounty with no feeling of guilt toward my fellow prisoners. I have since blamed myself for such selfishness, but then it was simply a matter of life or death.

The transportation of prisoners of the '45 across the ocean was not undertaken by the Crown or the Royal Navy. It was private business, and about a thousand of us were sold to the American plantations, under pain of death should we return. By "sold," I mean indentured for seven years, to work for merchants or planters. After the seven years, during which time we received only our keep, we were on our own. The transportation was arranged by two merchants, Samuel Smith of London and Richard Gildart of Liverpool, who received five pounds a head for the sea voyage and seven more pounds on the transferral of our indenture. It was a profitable business for them.

While awaiting a ship we were housed at Tilbury, in the fort's powder galleries. By the time a ship had been found and the western sea was thought to be free of French privateers, we'd been plundered down to a loincloth or a ragged shred of tartan. God alone knows how we survived the eight weeks aboard ship, sucking air through chinks in the timber and drinking foul water from buckets used by the sailors as latrines. Yet most of us lived to stumble on deck into daylight at a port called Wecomica on the Chesapeake Bay, there to be examined and sold off like animals or black slaves.

# 14

*The Jacob Randall place west of Cowpens*
*Early morning,* OCTOBER 7, 1780

A night of cold drizzle has played the devil with our flint-locks and we have halted here to dry and prime them afresh. Jacob Randall, no kin of mine, is being closely watched, for his politics are unknown.

The Tories, as expected, have moved to the steep summit of Kings Mountain, four miles hence, and though we are aware of no reinforcements slipping through our lines to his aid, Major Patrick Ferguson boldly defies God and the Devil to dislodge him.

I have perhaps no more than minutes to conclude this journal, minutes to treat of years, the first three of which I spent alone serving out my indenture helping supervise slaves on a tobacco plantation. Then Peggy braved the ocean to join me. We had exchanged letters, and it is not as though she left that much behind, for though the Sinclairs had never declared for Charlie they were persecuted along with the rest of us. As soon as Peggy arrived we were wed in the plantation chapel, and I maintain to this day that

Peggy Sinclair is the best thing that has happened to me in this life.

My indenture finally served out, I was presented with a gun and ax for good behavior, and we struck off on our own toward the mountainous frontier of western Virginia down toward the North Carolina line, for it reminded us both of home, which neither of us has seen since. In their letters my own family spoke of coming to America, but they never did, at first because my father was unwell. He never recovered physically or spiritually from the '45. There was much hardship in Scotland, particularly in the winters. Even the British garrison at Fort William knew starvation and death in that white world of snow and rolling mist.

When my father died no clan bard took his place, for there was no clan chief to call on him, and so the MacDonald pipes of Glencoe were forever stilled. As far as I know, my mother, should she live, and my sister Mary abide there still, keeping the black cattle, but it has not been since before this war of independence began that I have heard from them.

You may well ask what became of Prince Charlie. When he went off to Europe it was not to pout and brood like his father before him. Charlie yearned for revenge, without, I suppose, any consideration of the consequences to Scotland should his plans fail again. They did not fail, for they never came to pass. Fate had long since abandoned Charlie. In 1747 his brother Henry became a Catholic cardinal, which did much to disenchant Charlie's Protestant followers. A year later, England and France signed a treaty at Aix-la-Chapelle that required Charlie to be expelled from France. Not that he gave up, but his efforts to raise an army became a hysterical game. He traveled far and wide through Europe wearing beards and false noses to disguise himself, assumed a dozen names, and set chairs hung with bells around his bed at night lest assassins surprise him.

In 1750 he joined Stuart plotters in London—disguised of course—and handed out rings bearing the motto "Look, Love, and Follow." Naught came of this, and back in Europe he was reunited with Clementina Walkinshaw, who had served him kindly in the '45. Their daughter Charlotte was born in 1753. Two years later, war broke out again between England and France. Some elderly Jacobites rallied once again, but Charlie, increasingly cynical, refused to lead them unless France gave him twenty-five thousand troops. This France could not do, since they were losing the war. The years rolled by. In 1766 old "James III" died, and our Charlie became the Stuart pretender in exile. Meanwhile in London, King George III had come to the throne, more English than Charlie would ever be. By now the clan system was gone from Scotland, and no man capable of wielding a broadsword could recall a Stuart on the throne. So Charlie lived on in Rome, the only place that would tolerate him now.

You may not credit this, but there was a plot afoot in Boston to set Prince Charles up as king in the colonies. But Charlie was a drunk by this time, with his heart set not upon the distant colonies, nor upon Scotland which had loved him, but on England. They say that Charlie has never lost the belief that what he desires most will finally come true. Perhaps I'm like that, too. I smile sometimes, and I know that no one has ever died—not my father, not Angus Og; that we are all there again, ready to raise the banner at Glenfinnan once more.

I believe that is why I am here now after more than thirty years, part farmer, part hunter, part soldier, fighting for Charlie yet again and the freedom he promised us. Madness, maybe, but not so daft, it seems to me, as were all those Scottish exiles who took the Sassenachs' side and joined a royal regiment to fight for King George. Yet such is the legion we must fight today, Tories from a background like our own and led by a Scot for all of that, Patrick Ferguson, who is said to be an arrogant but brave soldier. Yes, for me it is the same fight, and I do smile when I think of the many ready to raise the same old cry once more, eager to carry it farther until this new world of ours is free of kings and princes entirely and may cast across the frontiers its undying light. There are no pipers now, but our drummers beat assembly. Kings Mountain looms before us. May God bless our cause. May He bless you all. And yes, with all that's gone before, I still believe in victory.

# POSTSCRIPT

Colin Randall MacDonald survived until after the War of 1812, though Kings Mountain was his last battle. It was a resounding victory for the American patriots and, though small as battles go, was a turning point for the southern campaign, which led to Cornwallis's final surrender at Yorktown a year later.

The leaders at Kings Mountain—ironically, both Scottish—were less fortunate than most of their men. Patrick Ferguson, leading a desperate charge, fell in a hail of rifle bullets and is buried on the wooded slopes of Kings Mountain. Colonel William Campbell, the rebel leader, survived the battle and was elevated to brigadier for his achievement, only to die the following summer of a heart attack. His patriot army, the self-styled "Over Mountain Men," melted away. But for them, Kings Mountain was not the end but a new beginning.

At this time, Prince Charles Edward Stuart still had eight years to live. It has been said that those whom the gods love die young, but Charlie lived on, the reigning King of Highland Hearts (*Righ nan Gaidheal*), though he had done the Highlands irreparable harm. At the time it was seen otherwise. His supporters regarded it as their duty to regain the crown, which they felt belonged to the Stuarts by divine right.

Though long lamenting the bloodbath left behind, Charles assumed no responsibility for it. He presumed leadership because men chose to follow, but he never accepted that they followed because he led. In his declining years he wept for lost majesty but never for the tragedy of the clans. He drank himself into oblivion because he could not lead Scotsmen into glory, but never because he wished Prince Charlie's Year had never happened. He died in Rome on the thirtieth of January, 1788. All he had ever yearned for was the crown of Great Britain.

The archaic Highland life-style was certainly doomed in the long run, but the Stuart pretenders to the throne finished the job in a hurry. Following the defeat at Culloden, many of the clan chiefs were hanged or exiled. It became unlawful to play the bagpipe or to wear the kilt. Tartans were sewn up into ludicrous breeches and then all but vanished. Touring the Highlands nearly thirty years after Culloden, Dr. Samuel Johnson could say, "They have created a desert and have called it Peace." Such a comment suggests a growing sympathy and a beginning of the so-called Highland Romance, which would more than restore Scotland to respectability. But it would soon be a very different Scotland. The warrior clans were broken, and the men who had drawn their broadswords for Prince Charles had been exiled or cajoled into the British army for their fighting spirit. Those who remained fared little better. They were less valuable on the land as tenant farmers than were the sheep, which replaced the herds of black cattle. A century after Culloden, when army recruiters came to Scotland to enlist men to fight in the Crimean War, they were told, "Since you have preferred sheep to men, let sheep defend you." By this time, the Stuarts and the clans were gone forever.

# A Brief Note on the Succession to the British Crown Which Led to the Jacobite Rebellions of 1715 and 1745

When England broke with the Catholic Church of Rome during the reign of Henry VIII, deep religious divisions arose between the newly outlawed Catholics and those who followed the Protestant faiths. Religious persecutions marked the reigns of Henry VIII's two daughters, Mary Tudor and Elizabeth I. The schism between the two faiths and the struggle between king and parliament for power continued from the sixteenth to the eighteenth century, culminating in the Jacobite Rebellions, when the modern concept of constitutional monarchy proved more successful than the old order represented by the last of the Stuart claimants to the throne, Bonnie Prince Charlie.

Mary Stuart, Queen of Scots, was a Catholic, the daughter of the king of Scotland and his French queen. Her first husband was the heir to the throne of France. Her second husband, Lord Darnley, was a Scot and a Protestant. Their son became King James VI of Scotland. Mary was executed by order of Elizabeth I of England.

After the death of Elizabeth I of England, a Protestant, with no heir, Mary Stuart's son, James VI of Scotland, became James I of England.

James I's son became Charles I of England and Scotland. In part because of Charles I's insistence on the divine right of kings and his French wife's Catholicism, civil war broke out. After the king's execution, Britain was governed by parliament and Oliver Cromwell.

After Cromwell's death the monarchy was restored, and Charles I's son became Charles II, who publicly upheld Protestantism but whose private sympathies were Catholic.

Charles II's brother succeeded him as James II of England. James II married Anne Hyde and had two daughters, Mary and Anne. Mary married the Protestant Prince William of Orange. James II, the last Stuart king, made no secret of his Catholicism and maintained the divine right of kings, leading to the Bloodless Revolution of 1688 and his exile.

James II's second wife was Mary of Modena. Their son, Prince James Francis Edward Stuart, who lived in exile in France and Italy, would have been King James III of England and James VIII of Scotland had the Stuarts remained on the throne. He was known as the Old Pretender by the Whig government in England and their supporters.

Prince James's son, born in Rome, was Prince Charles Edward Stuart, Bonnie Prince Charlie. Father and son sought to regain the British throne; James in 1708, 1715, and 1719, and Charles in 1745–1746 for his father. Their followers were called Jacobites, after the Latin for James, *Jacobus*. All rebellions to restore the Stuarts to the throne were failures, due in part to the Jacobites' lack of recognition of the success of the Hanoverian monarchy and the distrust by the majority of Britons of Catholicism and France, their traditional enemy. Both Stuarts were sheltered by the French court and promised military aid by France.

After James II had been deposed and exiled, his daughter Mary and her husband, William of Orange, jointly ruled Great Britain.

William and Mary were succeeded by Mary's younger sister, who became Queen Anne. Queen Anne died without living heirs, and the 1701 Act of Settlement made Sophia, the granddaughter of James I, the next Protestant heir to the throne.

Sophia was the wife of the elector of Hanover, a princely state in Germany. Their son became King George I of Great Britain. The Jacobite uprising of 1715 occurred during his reign. George I's son, George II, was king during the 1745 Jacobite Rebellion. The duke ("Butcher") of Cumberland was the son of George II. George III, who was king during the American Revolution, was the grandson of George II.

# GLOSSARY

AULD ALLIANCE   Long-term friendship between Scotland and France based in part on religion, royal marriage, and a common enemy—England.

BAIRN   A child, or a person of simple mind regardless of age.

BEAN NIGHE   A night spirit associated with death and evil tidings.

BELTANE FIRES   A May festival celebrating the coming of warm weather, during which fires are set.

BOTHY (OR BOTHIE)   Cottage for a common farmer.

BURN   A brook.

CEILIDH (PRONOUNCED "CAYLEE")   Singing, dancing, various entertainment in an organized setting.

CLAYMORE   Literally, "great sword." A sixteenth-century hand-and-a-half sword, though the later basket-hilted swords are often called claymores in Scotland.

CORRIE   A sheltered meadow. V., to gossip.

DIRK   Traditional Scottish dagger, serving for a weapon, hunting tool, and utility knife.

DOWIE   Sad, languid.

GALLOWAY   Highland pony or horse, originating in Galloway, Scotland.

HAGGIS   A sheep's maw (stomach) containing minced lungs, heart, and liver of sheep, mixed and cooked with oatmeal, suet, onions, salt, and pepper. Like a spicy sausage meat.

HUMBLIES   The lowest of the low, the ineffectual riffraff of a Highland army.

LAIRD   Lord, landlord of a house.

PIBROCH   Highland bagpipe music.

RANT   Literally, a rage; in this case, a fury of piping to encourage men to charge into battle.

SPORRAN   A Highlander's purse, worn about the waist.

TARGET   Also targe, a circular wood-based, leather-covered shield, sometimes tooled and studded with tacks, often having a protruding central metal spike.